DAY OF RECKONING

BY

CHARLES R. YOUNG

Day of Reckoning
Copyright: Charles R. Young
Published: August 2016
ISBN: 978-1533323798
Publisher: CreateSpace Independent Publishers

ALL RIGHTS RESERVED. No part of this book may be reproduced or transmitted for resale or use by any party other than the individual purchaser, who is the sole authorized user of this information. Purchaser is authorized to use any of the information in this publication for his or her own use ONLY. All other reproduction or transmission, in any form or by any means, electronic or mechanical, including photocopying, recording, or by any information storage or retrieval system, is prohibited without express written permission from Charles R. Young.

DISCLAIMER: This is a work of fiction. Names, characters, businesses, places, events and incidents are either the products of the author's imagination or used in a fictitious manner. Any resemblance to actual persons, living or dead, or actual events is purely coincidental.

Author headshot photo credit: Sam Sarkis Photography.

Published by: CreateSpace Independent Publishers

© Charles R. Young, 2016

I dedicate this book to Debbie Carson with much love and appreciation. She always gives me unconditional encouragement, support, and motivation when needed.

THE BEGINNING

Baharak, Afghanistan

The mountainous air at 10:30 p.m. in mid-November in the border town of Baharak, just east of Kabul, Afghanistan was cold, dark, and exceptionally quiet. Three Afghani guards stood outside a stone hedge with a large closed wooden gate surrounding a brick home. Each of the guards held a loaded AK-47. The automatic machine guns were unintended gifts left by the Russians as spoils of their war with Afghanistan from 1979-1989. The guards were alert for any unexpected movements around the perimeter of the house. They were expecting a very special guest and security precautions were at a high.

At about 10:45 p.m., they sighted the dust trail of fast moving vehicles heading toward the residential destination under watch. As they neared, the sound of the powerful SUV engines began to echo throughout the village. They arrived and once identified, were immediately passed through the opened security gate. Three black, bullet-proofed, Mercedes SUVs came to a halt and six armed guards emerged, forming a protective ring around the vehicles. One of the guards opened the back door on the second car and an Arabic man in full ethnic garb stepped out. Who he was, where he was from, and the purpose of his visit were question marks, but it was obvious he was a major figure, at the very least a representative of an existing power, one whose middle of the night meetings were conducted under concealment for good reason.

He entered the house with two of his personal guards and was greeted by five men wearing Afghani robes and hats. After the usual cordial greetings were completed, the entourage moved into the larger living room furnished with a long, rectangular wooden table and chairs. An offer of food and drink was declined by the guest of honor.

His presentation addressed the need to step up the suicide bombings and other disruptive political activities on an international level. He further explained that random acts of violence would effectively serve to break down the infrastructure of those nations considered hostile. A continued argument was made to defend the violent actions as militarily disadvantaged responses by third world powers against the super powers. "The word 'terrorism,'" he said, "was nothing more than a westernized term for retaliation by oppressed nations that have been targeted by massive military forces." He went on to explain how the American military and financial support of Israel has been and always will be an affront to most Middle Eastern countries.

There were no actual details discussed about who was funding or supplying the proposed retaliation attacks. No specific targets were mentioned; those present already had their own assigned areas. At the conclusion of the meeting, the guest of honor handed each man a sealed manila envelope. In it were the necessary details of suggested targets, religious groups, and political factions, and a proposed timetable for initiating the actions discussed. The farewell greetings were made and the SUV convoy departed into the darkness of night. The business was done. It was time for action.

CHAPTER 1

Chicago, Illinois

BOOM! In one shattering moment, the explosion rocked the entire city block and changed the lives forever of those within its walls. Sid's Delicatessen, once a local legend in Jewish cuisine, was now blown-out bits of rubble and smoke. Worst of all were the sounds of agonizing pain, the cries for help by those injured and burned by the explosion, in contrast to the eerie quiet of death. As the cloud of smoke and airborne particles settled, a tortured landscape revealed the injured—conscious and unconscious—dusted with a flour-like layer of dust and larger debris. Body parts were strewn about, lying in pools of blood with human tissue sprayed against destroyed surfaces.

Within minutes of the explosion, sirens could be heard at a distance. Fire trucks, police cars, and emergency medical vehicles all sped to the restaurant's site on E.59th Street. The sirens shrilled as they approached, silent to survivors of the blast. Blown out ear drums and shock had obliterated their hearing and created a miasma of confusion and fear as those who were able, moved from the site of destruction towards the light of day. Survivors were seen assisting others, giving care to friends and loved ones, and crawling or limping towards the safety of daylight.

On that day in Chicago, at what was once Sid's Delicatessen, survival was the only goal. Questions about the cause or extent of the damage would come later, and those who lived would be deeply scarred by the trauma for the rest of their lives.

Tel Aviv, Israel / Three Months Earlier

The Director of Covert Operations, a special division of the Israeli Mossad, sat patiently waiting for his requested conference with the Prime Minister and other high-ranking political officials. His identification badge read Alon Levy, with a grade four security clearance. It meant Levy could go almost anywhere in Israel and talk to high-ranking officials without seeking special permission. His fellow Mossad agents referred to him as Alon to his face, but always saw him as a hard-ass in the operative field. When trouble arose, and it often did, you thanked God if Alon Levy was with you.

An attractive young woman in her early 40s stepped out of the conference door and announced it was time for Alon to join the meeting. Upon entering, Alon nodded at several of the attendees; he knew most everyone there and joined them at the conference table.

The Prime Minister spoke first. "Alon," he said, "how are you and the children? Again, I want to offer my condolence for the loss of your wife. She was a good woman and a loss to all of us."

"Thank you, sir,"

"Alon," the Prime Minister said, "we are interested in your present assessment of Middle Eastern planned, subsidized, and/or anticipated terrorist acts. We are particularly interested in activities that target Jewish population groups both in and outside of Israel."

Alon opened a plastic briefcase and removed a chart marked "confidential" in red letters. He scanned the contents though he knew the information it held. "First of all, sir," he began, "our field sources indicate there are greater political pressures to push for an increase in international Jewish terrorist activities in the very near future. The consensus of opinions seems to be that these anti-Jewish strikes are not supported financially, militarily or verbally by any particular government. Rather, they are being subsidized by smaller, but powerful radicalized factions behind the scenes. Now, understand me when I say our neighboring countries, although not publicly supporting this movement, will do nothing to stop it. And that pretty much sums up what we have thus far."

The Minister of Defense spoke. "Alon, I'd like your opinion. How do you envision the magnitude of the terrorist strikes? Will they be large events, political assassinations, missile attacks? How do you think the attacks will take place?"

"Gentlemen, I have no data or evidence from any reliable source to even offer an educated guess. Our only viable indication is that these preemptive attacks will soon be on the increase and will target Jewish and non-Jewish groups on an international level. Their main objective appears to be to destabilize American-Israeli relations and in particular, the political and financial support of the Jewish state by the Western powers. A second objective would be to use random terrorist attacks to create fear as a deterrent against utilizing governmental sanctions and/or military actions against the Middle Eastern countries."

The Prime Minister responded, "Alon, how do you think these attacks will occur? Don't tell us about a lack of credible evidence. Give us your damn opinion and forget the politically correct answers. We are family, friends, and colleagues, so say what you mean, what you believe. All of us here respect your opinion."

"Okay. First of all, I believe the terrorist attacks will be small scale random actions with suicide bombings at the head of the list. Larger attacks would more likely require governmental support, and retaliatory actions would be too costly so I don't see that route as viable. Terrorist groups do not favor surviving activists. Suicide missions are more likely."

One of the other seated leaders at the table interjected, "Assuming your assessment is accurate, what can we do about it?"

Alon Levy, who had thus far responded with confidence, hesitated. "Gentlemen, I am not sure my response will satisfy anyone. How do we stop someone wearing a jacket lined with explosives from walking into a restaurant, theatre, or coffee shop and setting it off? The worst part is that he or she believes the act is not only justified, but a mark of valor. Such an enemy is nearly impossible to defeat. The only answer that makes sense to me is to identify and target the source of the act. Cut off a tentacle from the octopus and it still moves about, but you destroy the head and the beast dies."

The Prime Minister looked at Alon and replied, "Set up a task force. Make it your mission to locate and/or identify the supporting groups. Then, when we have the information we need, let's kill the beast!"

CHAPTER 2

Israel/Gaza Border: Three months earlier

Saran Kassab and his two fellow workers waited in line for their turn to pass through the security gate into Israel. The standard of life within the PLO section was far below that of most American inner-city areas. Jobs, food, daily commodities, and basic living standards were, in many cases, unobtainable. Worse was the generalized feeling of being prisoners controlled by the Israeli government. The Palestinians felt neglected, mistreated, and persecuted by an armed Jewish military force with no end in sight. The PLO population was a unique problem; they were a people with no national identity, no recognizable leadership, and no neighboring country offering to absorb them and address their problems.

As Saran approached the border security checkpoint, he became increasingly aware of the cold dispassionate manner in which the guard addressed those in line. *If only the tables were turned,* he thought. The Israeli Jews were in control now, but Saran told himself that one day soon, things would be very different. At least, that is what he and his friends had heard on a daily basis at the training camp sessions during the previous year in Pakistan.

The guard looked at Saran and without any show of emotion or concern muttered, "Papers." Saran showed his work visa and prepared to pass through the designated gate. The guard passed the work papers back without a word, then turned to the next person in line. Saran felt those in line were like dogs or beggars. *Wait in line,* he thought to himself. *Be quiet, respectful, and obedient, and you may be given a cookie treat by the benevolent Israeli guard.* Someday, Saran swore to himself, he would return the favor!

The three friends went to the same workplace, handling custodial and landscape assignments at an Israeli private school facility. Their pay gave them buying power at the PLO market centers. On occasion, they would purchase Israeli goods, but preferred to spend the money with their own people and feed their present home economy. Saran remembered bitterly how one day he bought a bag of Israeli assorted fruits to take home to his family. At the security checkpoint, one of the guards helped himself to half the fruit and offered the rest around to his armed colleagues. When Saran asked him to pay for the fruit, the guard laughed and told him to pass through the gate before he decided to take more fruit.

However, during the last six months or so, Saran also had another job that didn't pay as much, but was more gratifying. He and his two friends had been recruited to meet at someone's home and work for two hours, twice a week on a special project. They would sit at a table conversing, listening to music or eating, while applying detonating devices to explosives. Once activated, these devices were capable of being set off by cell phones from a distance. The three young men were trained to do the electronic link-up, but the process was tedious and required several hours of time to complete a single one. Saran and his friends knew the explosives were made to be worn in a vest or jacket; the concept of suicide bombing was assumed. They dared not ask any questions.

Saran knew his evening work was dangerous. Regardless, for the first time in years he felt he was doing something of substantial value for his homeland. He had no idea when or where the explosive units would be used and didn't care. He knew he was contributing in a small way to striking back at Israeli oppression. Saran, as well as the others, had all taken an oath not to discuss their work with anyone.

Saran's family lived in a small community on the outskirts of Cairo. His father was a strict disciplinarian, frequently unfair in his childrearing, as well as unemotional and unaffectionate. He worked long hours repairing furniture. Saran's mother was an Egyptian jewel who sold baked goods in the market square for additional income. Together, their income provided a middle-class lifestyle and the possibility of future opportunities for their two sons. Saran was the oldest and did not get along well with his father. Walid, his younger brother by three years, was more adaptable and able to coexist in peace with the man. Walid was not as street smart nor as proficient in manual labor as Saran, but he was academically gifted, and often dreamed of becoming an engineer or scientist. His mother supported his academic accomplishments and vowed to do anything to assist his further education.

Saran left his home in 2012 at the age of 19 and moved into the Palestinian area to live with his uncle, Faruz. He appreciated the opportunity to stay, and got along with his uncle fairly well even though Saran knew he was far overpaying his share of the living costs. Many weeks every *shekel* he earned by manual labor went to cover his housing and food expenses. His evening work with the explosives paid for extras and Saran kept it a secret from the uncle. He began to get a better sense of the PLO's viewpoint on Israeli oppression, frequently witnessing the effects of Israeli military control, social and political injustices, and day-to-day mistreatment of his fellow citizens. Hatred of the Israeli presence and its ruling control became a festering wound that worsened with time.

CHAPTER 3

As the youngest of the three men working at the evening explosive assembly site, Saran was frequently sent out to pick up food and drinks for the others. One such night proved to be both a blessing and a nightmare. Saran left the house to get a pizza and beer. For Saran and his coworkers, pizza was perhaps the best commodity devised by the western world. The walk back to the house was a short one and he noticed with concern that the area around the house was cordoned off by armed Israeli guards. A small, growing crowd of Arab residents had formed. As Saran stood in the crowd, he could see snipers on the building rooftops in the front and rear of the house. Another group of Israelis gathered about fifty yards to the side, and a smaller force of three was positioned at the rear. This was a Mossad operation. Saran knew his friends in the house were in grave danger.

He sent a text to one of his friends with a simple message. "Mossad agents surround the house. Surrender without fight if necessary. Hide items if possible."

Saran did not expect a reply and there wasn't one. He watched in astonishment as one of his friends raced out of the back door in a panic to escape. Before the surrounding agents could apprehend the young man, two high-powered sniper bullets hit him directly in the chest. Blood spurted from his wounds as he dropped and rolled down the last few steps of the stairway. He was dead before he hit the ground. Within seconds of the attempted escape, the remaining coworker came out of the front door with his hands held high in the air. Israeli agents were everywhere. They cuffed Saran's friend and rushed him into a guarded vehicle. The dead young man on the ground was promptly zipped into a body bag and loaded into one of the vehicles. Meanwhile, other agents moved into the house and retrieved the explosives, detonation devices, and the suicide vests. The crowd of citizens held back by armed Israelis grew restless; sporadic anti-Semitic outcries filled the air. Then as quickly and quietly as they had come, the agents and their team left the area. No sirens sounded and the vacating military force was silent as well. Flashing lights on their vehicles and the convoy-like exit pattern were the only signs of their presence.

Saran stood motionless in the crowd, visibly shaken by what had taken place. The Israelis had obviously been informed of the ongoing household activities and responded predictably and professionally. The sight of a his friend shot in the chest and tumbling down a stairway like a sack of potatoes was shocking and obscene. He knew he needed to leave the scene for a safer location, unencumbered by food and drink so he nudged the middle-aged man next to him and passed off the pizza and beer as a gift. Saran collected his thoughts. His primary concern was the Israeli surveillance of the house. Saran assumed it would not take long for their interrogation of the man they captured to reveal Saran's name and the address of his uncle's home.

As he wandered through the neighborhood he used his cell phone to call his uncle. After a short, honest explanation of the incident, his uncle told him not to return to the house. In terse language, his uncle told Saran he had abused his visit, and jeopardized the safety and security of the family. "Do not come here!" His uncle demanded. "You are no longer welcome." Saran swallowed hard, knowing he could not return.

Saran's second concern was his brother, Walid. While he felt nothing for his father and only mild concern for his mother, he did have affectionate feelings for his brother. A year prior, he had convinced him to attend a six-month anti-Israeli training camp. Walid rejected the Islamic ideologies and left after completing his instructional program. Saran was now concerned that once the Israelis had his name, they would follow the family ties to Cairo and investigate Walid's past. They would call it radical Islamic terrorist training and anyone the least bit connected to it would be considered a hostile enemy.

Saran called Walid. In few words, he advised him to leave the country for a while. Saran said he planned to move around and become a lost soul in the local Arabic community wherever he wandered. He wished Walid well and ended his conversation with a traditional and meaningful Islamic blessing.

CHAPTER 4

Egypt

It took Saran only a couple of weeks to tire of his fugitive status. He assumed the Israeli authorities had his name and knew of his recent participation assembling explosives. Despite any concrete evidence, Saran suspected the Israelis were pursuing him. His lifestyle was meager and his funds were running thin. Saran went into a neighborhood coffee shop and paid the extra charge for using the store's laptop. He contacted one of the recruiting sites with whom he had originally trained. Saran was instructed to remain at the coffee shop; someone would be sent to meet with him.

One hour later a tall, lanky man in his mid-thirties entered the shop. After making eye contact with Saran, their meeting was on. For thirty minutes they spoke about Saran's recent training and experience with the Israeli authorities. Saran reiterated his hatred for the Israelis and for the way they were treating his fellow countrymen. It didn't take long for Saran to hear the offer he was hoping to receive; his safety and security by the Islamic organization in exchange for his loyalty and work. Free housing would be provided in return for Saran's weekly work as a member of the hand-carried explosive bomb unit. His job, as before, would be to assemble explosives with their detonators for use by suicide bombers. The man told Saran to report to his new home for work in 36 hours, which allowed ample time for Saran to see his parents and bid them a proper farewell.

Saran returned to his home in Egypt and was greeted at the front door by his tearfully happy mother. His father, Rafal, seated at the kitchen table, was less emotional. Saran was excited to hear the news that Walid had been awarded a scholarship to the University of Chicago in America. He was there now studying hard to become an engineer. Saran was proud of his brother and hoped he would be successful in his studies. They made small talk for a while and then sat down for a home-cooked meal.

During dinner Saran told of his experiences in Palestine and how the local people were treated by the Israeli border guards and authorities. He explained his work assembling explosive hand-carried bombs, leaving his parents sitting speechless at the table.

His father interrupted Saran and spoke with an unfriendly firmness. "Saran, what would ever possess you to involve yourself with such people? Who raised you to think that killing people is acceptable in the eyes of Allah?"

"Father," Saran replied, "the Israeli devils should die and their government's oppressive control over our Arab brothers must end. My existence on this earth is committed to assisting in the eradication of these people. I hate them all!"

"Fool! You sound like someone reading from a prepared script. We never raised you to hate with such passion nor to want to harm innocent men, women, and children. Yes, we have differences with the politics of Israel, but setting off bombs and killing people are not legitimate answers to our problems. Reconsider your thoughts and plans, and do so before you commit to any particular course of action that could get you or others killed."

"Your reactions to my feelings are not a surprise, father. You have always been a pacifist, a sheep that goes where the herder leads you. You think only of your own household, and fail to see the injustice and oppression around you. Well, I do see it and have pledged to do something about it."

"No son of mine is going to make bombs to kill innocent people and say it was Allah's will. Those are not the teachings of the Quran!"

"Well, this son is going to and there is nothing you can do or say to persuade me otherwise."

Saran's mother broke into the conversation, "Please, please stop this senseless argument. Eat your dinner and we will discuss this matter later."

Rafal slammed his open hand on the tabletop, quieting the room. "Saran," he said. "If you do this thing, you are no longer my son, nor will you be welcome in this house!"

A cry burst from Saran's mother. "Don't speak of such things," she pleaded. "Saran is our son and this is his home. Never say things to close the door on our own blood."

"Forget it, mother. The way father thinks and acts, he would probably be happier living in Israel with the Jews and other westerners."

"Enough!" his father shouted, and stood up. "You can sit at this table, eat your dinner, and talk with your mother. I am done eating with you and listening to your poisonous thoughts. Tomorrow morning, pack your things and leave this house. There will be no reason for you ever to return." Rafal strode out of the house to let his feelings cool.

Saran ate in silence as his mother sat and cried. Saran always saw his father as a weak man incapable of meaningful action and his mother as a subservient spouse, raised to serve her husband and take care of the offspring.

Rafal wandered alone through the side streets of the neighborhood. He stopped for a few moments to watch the young children playing soccer on the cobblestone streets. He walked along watching the local residents file into restaurants for dinner and the store owners close their shops. Saran's father felt no love for the Israelis, but murdering civilians for ideological or religious reasons was neither a reasonable nor viable answer. People were people. Children in Tel-Aviv played soccer, their families went to neighboring restaurants for peaceful meals, and store owners operated similar shops regardless of their nationalities. Then, the thought of his own son making explosives for suicide bombers took control of his mind. He decided that as a parent, a peaceful Egyptian citizen, and as a caring member of the human race, it was his responsibility to stop his son from pursuing such a course of action. The thought of turning his son in to the local Egyptian authorities was repulsive. Yet, at least incarceration would keep him secure. Saran's safety superseded Rafal's own family needs and unfortunately, would leave his future relationship with Saran questionable.

With new determination he walked into a nearby police station and sat down with an officer. After describing the situation in general terms without giving anyone's name, he inquired as to the probable length of prison time involved. The answer was two or three years depending upon the individual's past criminal record and other such factors. Rafal then gave his son's name and address, and told them Saran planned to leave the next morning. The officer assembled two other guards and with the father, they set out to pick up Saran.

The arrest procedure went smoothly. Saran was handcuffed and escorted out the front door towards a waiting police vehicle as another officer held back his hysterical mother. Saran gave an icy stare to his father, who mirrored it back at his son. Each communicated their feelings without words. It would be a long time before Saran worked with explosives for terrorist distribution again.

CHAPTER 5

Chicago, Illinois

Sid's Delicatessen on E. 59th Street, in close proximity to the University of Chicago, was a well-known, well-loved establishment that specialized in corned beef, hot pastrami, and turkey club sandwiches. Students, professors and patrons from all over the area would congregate at Sid's and wait for one of the twenty or so chairs in the restaurant. Sid's was not fancy; no music of any kind played in the background. Instead, diners ate to the cacophony of the patrons as they conversed, laughed, and called to acquaintances at the other tables. Sid's Delicatessen was on the corner of a busy intersection. Its large paneled windows faced the street on two sides and were outlined by old red brick blocks that showed 40 years of wear and tear. The restaurant was not revered for its decor, quality service staff, or sophisticated food presentation. You went to Sid's for good, three-inch thick deli sandwiches, waitresses who had no time for small talk, and good times with friends. No bills were given to the customers at the end of the meal. You told the cashier what you had and paid the amount quoted. Sid's attracted customers from all walks of life and religious persuasions, and as one might expect from its geography and menu, it was a favorite gathering place for Jewish patrons.

In Chicago, February winter days could chill a polar bear. On this day, the weather was worse than merely cold—it was oppressive. The air temperature was seven degrees and the wind chill factor brought that down to 16 below zero. The streets of Chicago were busy as ever with traffic, pedestrians, and store fronts operating in a business-as-usual manner. Every time a store or restaurant front door opened, the escaping heat vaporized into a cloud. The Midwestern city was prepared to deal with the winter elements and so were its residents.

The five block walk from Sonya Levy's off-campus apartment to Sid's Delicatessen normally took 15 minutes, but today, the cold air, the frigid winds, and the congested sidewalks made the walk seem longer. Sonya's cheeks were red from the cold wind as it blew against her face and left an uncomfortable surface burn. She was meeting a friend for lunch, and she walked faster to avoid being late. Sonya Levy was 19 years old, born and raised in Israel, and had been living in the States for the last three years. She was a pre-law student majoring in liberal arts and an academic high achiever. Sonya was bilingual, politically liberal, and embraced strong moral values. She was attractive, too, with a nicely proportioned figure and a smile that caught the attention of others. Her smooth skin had the golden-brown complexion characteristic of her Middle Eastern origin, which was set off by a mane of long black hair. All in all, Sonya Levy was quite a package. She loved people, knew what she wanted in her future, and had a genuine verve for life.

She was raised in a strict, conservative Jewish home in Haifa. Her mother, an elementary school teacher, had died of leukemia when Sonya was 16. Her father, Alon Levy, was overly involved in his work and often away, yet found time to be with his daughter when she needed him. At six feet two inches, and 215 pounds, he was muscular as a pit bull and had a similar temperament, all of which melted away when he hugged her. Alon was a prominent and active officer in the Israeli secret service, Mossad. His past experiences could fill a book, if such things could be discussed. When Sonya's mother died, Alon took it hard and experienced bouts of depression and loneliness. He exchanged angry outbursts with his son, Nadev, over political issues and current government actions. In Israel, family traditions and values were frequently more important to those of previous generations than they were to the younger members of society. Nadev held liberal viewpoints about geopolitical issues that grated on his father. Alon's very existence was to protect Israel and its inhabitants from foreign threats at any cost and by any means. Nadev rarely agreed with his father about political issues and frequently saw Israel as the oppressor, insensitive to the Palestinian plight and the concerns of most of the neighboring countries. Increasingly, political issues" were driving father and son apart. Sonya leaned towards her father's views while remaining close to her brother.

Sonya hurried to Sid's Delicatessen to meet her friend, Denise, who was in her English class at school and also interested in law. The two studied together and had become good friends. Denise's high school sweetheart attended Duke, and in a gesture of kindness, Denise assumed the self-appointed role of finding a suitable partner for Sonya. At first, Denise wrongly assumed Sonya would only consider dating a Jewish man. Sonya would often talk about her father with Denise and the two of them would giggle at the thought of her taking a gentile to Israel to meet her father. Sonya mused, "I'd have to wonder whom Dad would kill first....me or the boyfriend!"

The cold wind had picked up. Sonya's nose was freezing and she wished for a warmer hat. As she pulled open the glass door and walked into Sid's, she was hit with a welcomed blast of warm air accompanied by the mouth-watering aroma of cooked corned beef, pastrami, and fresh sliced hot rye bread. In the cozy chaos people shouted, dishes clanged, and the cash register sang its tune. She heard her name and spotted Denise in a corner booth seated across from a young man. He was good looking with a dark complexion, and appeared to be about the same age. As Sonya approached, he immediately stood up and helped Sonya remove her heavy coat. As he hung it on the back of her chair, Denise began the introductions.

"Sonya, I want you to meet a friend of mine, Walid Kassab. He is in my history class and he's from Egypt. Now, I want the two of you to be friends and not try to kill each other. Is that possible?"

Grinning at Denise's comments, Sonya and Walid shook hands and waited for the other to begin a conversation. Sonya won the honors.

"Walid, what part of Egypt are you from and what brings you here?"

He smiled and replied, "I'm from a small town outside of Cairo. I came to the States on an engineering scholarship. The university has a great reputation for its science and engineering program. What about you?"

Sonya answered as if Denise were at another table. "I was born in Haifa. I came to Chicago three years ago to attend the pre-law program."

"Hey, guys" Denise interrupted. "I'm here too, and I'm hungry. What do you say we order some food and then continue with the chat?"

After the waitress took their order, Sonya and Walid continued their conversation.

"Tell me, Sonya", he said, "why law, and why leave Israel to attend a university here?"

Sonya considered how to answer. "I was raised in a house where right and wrong, good and evil, and justice were a big part of our daily lives. The establishment and enforcement of laws are important to me, and good lawyers are always needed."

"Did you say that at your law school interview?"

Sonya dropped her smile. "You asked a question and I gave you an honest answer. As far as leaving Israel is concerned, I needed some time away on my own. I fully intend to return after graduation."

"Sorry," Walid said. "I didn't mean to be unpleasant."

Between bites of her sandwich, Denise remarked, "Sonya, why don't you tell Walid the real scoop on why you needed some time away from home for a while?"

"Well," Sonya said, "let's just say my father can be a little overbearing. He and my brother, Nadev, are frequently on the outs with each other. Nadev lives in an apartment with two other friends, but when he comes to visit, he often upsets my dad by opening his mouth about certain issues. I suspect he does it on purpose. You see, my dad works for the government. He's a very fair and honest man, but he can be quite difficult when he gets angry."

"What about you, Walid? What's your story?"

"In Egypt, I sold fruit and vegetables from a street cart in Cairo. My parents were middle-income earners and always encouraged me to get an education. They put me in a private school where I learned English. I did well in the honors program and was exposed to the science curriculum. I'm close to my older brother, Saran. We have different aspirations in life. He respects education, but prefers manual labor jobs where he is free to roam and move from one site to another. I was lucky and got a scholarship to the University of Chicago undergraduate school and I saved up enough money to pay some of the living expenses. My parents and relatives helped finance the rest of my educational and travel costs."

Sonya lit up with excitement and with a full smile blurted out, "Oh, my God, I almost forgot to mention my most exciting news. My brother, Nadev, is planning on visiting me for two weeks at the end of February! Isn't that great? Denise, you're really going to enjoy him. He's a great guy and, Walid, you'll like him, too. Just don't get him started on the subject of politics."

The three students ate and talked for over an hour. The chemistry was right. Even though their backgrounds were wildly different, they friendships solidified. They talked about their parents, the passing of Sonya's mother and its impact upon her father. They talked briefly about political and ethnic differences, and relaxed discovering no one was particularly radical in his or her views. It was Denise's habit to throw in a final statement of neutrality and to remind everyone that as an American Catholic, her short-cut answer to peace in the Middle East was that everyone should convert to Catholicism. If only life could be that simple.

Chapter 6

Over the next couple of months, the three college friends hung out together. They studied at the library, shared frequent meals, and vented their problems with each other. Before long, they grew to know each other in terms of what each one was thinking, how they felt about different issues, and what particular emotional buttons to avoid.

Sonya's brother, Nadev, would arrive soon for his visit. Sonya could hardly wait. Nadev had been to the States once, three years earlier. At that time, the Levy family had gone to New York for two weeks and left with a lifetime of wonderful memories and experiences. Alon had business meetings during the daytime, the specifics of which were never addressed. Sonya knew only that he was a guest lecturer on the subject of airport security and dealing with terrorism. During the day, Sonya, her mother, and Nadev went sightseeing, took organized tours, and shopped at the fancy malls. Periodic phone calls would come in from Alon to arrange dinner and evening entertainment. Sonya remembered that Nadev's main interest was how to wrangle private time to meet American girls. His good looks and Israeli accent attracted others at the college hangouts, but the tight family leash made outside social interactions difficult.

Everyone who knew Alon would sooner or later discover evidence of his unpredictable behavior. One evening during an after dinner walk on the New York trip, the family saw a homeless, one-legged, middle-aged man leaning up against a brick building. Alon told the family he would be right back and to wait where they were. He walked over to the man, crouched down, and asked how he was getting along. Nodding toward the missing leg, Alon asked, "War injury?" The man nodded in return and said he was a Vietnam War veteran. He had lost his family and home to bad times. Alon reached into his pocket and gave the man a hundred dollars.

"Are you kidding me?" the man asked when he saw the bill.

"No. Take the money and know it is a small token of gratitude for what you've done. You're a war hero, a good man, and should always be proud of the sacrifices you made for your country. I salute you," he said with a quick snap of his hand to his forehead.

"Bless you, man," the veteran kept repeating as Alon Levy walked back to his family.

The following day, the Levy family rode in a taxi taking their father to another meeting at the Hilton Hotel. Traffic was heavy and the cab ride was slow. Alon became increasingly anxious about being late for his appointment. As the car stood still in the traffic, a man darted out to the side of the car and began washing the windows with his squeegee. The driver lowered the window and leaned out. "Hey, squeegee, cut it out! These guys are in a hurry," he barked. The man continued to wash. "I said stop it!"

The light turned green and the squeegee man trotted alongside the cab as they crept along. Alon flung open the passenger door, jumped out of the cab, grabbed the squeegee, snapped it in two like a dry twig and thrust it back into the man's hands. "Leave now!" he said in a low voice between clenched teeth, "or this will happen to you!" The man scurried away.

That was Alon Levy. One minute, a soft spoken, even-tempered, super-sensitive guy with a big heart. The next minute, a wound-up, over-anxious, angry son-of-a-bitch coiled like a rattlesnake ready to strike. At 42, Alon, easily passed for a man in his early thirties. He was strong and had lightning fast reflexes. As an elite member of the Israeli secret service and a seasoned leader in their Special Forces unit, Alon was expertly trained and had a wide skill set. He could diffuse most detonators on the market, kill a man with a credit card, and interrogate a prisoner in ways not discussed in textbooks. In short, Alon Levy was a walking military machine you'd rather have as a friend than an enemy.

Alon was a happily married man for 21 years until his wife died of leukemia. Her passing hit him hard and threw him into intermittent bouts of depression. After a short period of time, he found himself being ordered into anger management counseling and private psychological sessions to address his problems. Certain family relationships became more pronounced. He adored his daughter Sonya, and in his eyes, she could do no wrong. But he and Nadev were like oil and water, continuing to grow apart personally, spiritually and ideologically. When they were together, they argued. Sonya found ways to calm them.

Sonya and Nadev rarely argued about anything. They adored each other and always tried to celebrate their accomplishments in life—big or small.

Nadev was excited to visit Sonya in Chicago and spend a couple of weeks at her campus apartment. Alon drove him to the airport.

"Nadev," Alon said, "do you have enough money or do you want me to give you some?"

"I'm fine. Thanks anyway."

"And you'll call me when you arrive?"

"Look, Dad," Nadev replied. "I am not moving to Chicago. I'm just visiting. I'm 21 years old...a man, not a child. I promise I'll call. Let go, will you?"

"You know," Alon snapped, "sometimes you can be one big asshole, but because you are my only son and leaving the country shortly, I will try to overlook your constant insensitivity."

The car pulled up to El-Al Airlines at the Ben Gurion Airport in Tel Aviv. Nadev reached in the back seat for his suitcase. "Dad, do me a favor please while I'm gone," he said.

"What's that?"

"Try to open your mind a little about the treatment of those Palestinian refugees and see if you can back off with that special Mossad treatment you and your colleagues specialize in."

Alon's anger rose to the surface and his face reddened. This time, Alon was determined not to bite the bait. He took an audible breath.

"Nadev," he said just above a whisper, "take your bag. Go visit your sister in Chicago. Have a wonderful time and keep in mind that when you return to Israel, your loving father and Mossad devil will be there to further harass and embarrass you."

The two said their good-byes, gave each other a brief hug, and went their separate ways. As Alon drove off, he shook his head. How and why had Nadev gotten to this point? His ideological transformation seemed to worsen with the death of his mother. Nadev was always the one with the controversial views and strange attitudes. And weren't children known for defying their parents? That's what the younger generation was all about—free thinking and open expressions with occasional periods of rationality and reasoning. Bottom line—he loved his children. They were going to spend two weeks together. Besides, he figured, after they lay me in my grave the kids will still have each other. He smiled at the comforting thought.

Chapter 7

Who knew the specific cause of upper respiratory infections? One thing was sure...the frigid winds of a Chicago winter were not helpful. Sonya came down with a nasty head cold that rapidly progressed into a flu-like condition with congestion, low-grade fever, chills, muscle aches, joint pains and general fatigue. Attending school classes was impossible when getting out of bed was an unmet challenge. Her friend Denise went grocery shopping and was kind enough to prepare several dinners so Sonya could stay in bed and not have to worry about food. Sonya figured she had plenty of time to recover before Nadev arrived.

At 11:30 a.m. Sonya was awakened by her cell phone playing a programmed symphonic melody.

She checked her caller ID. "Hi, Walid," she muttered with great effort.

"Yeah, it's me," he replied. "Missed you and your smile. How are you feeling this wonderful winter day in Chicago? Better I hope."

"Not so good, I'm afraid." Her voice gave away her physical condition. "I know this misery will break, but right now it's lousy!"

"Tell you what, Sonya," Walid said, "I'll stop at Sid's Deli and pick up a quart of chicken noodle soup and a quart of matzo ball soup. Ring me in and we'll sit around, have some soup and talk awhile. When you get tired of me, you can tell me to leave. What do you say?"

Sonya groaned. "Oh, I'd love the soup and your company, but I'd feel terrible if you caught this bug and got sick."

"Let me worry about that," he said. "I don't often get sick from hanging around others and after all, I don't expect we'll start a romance."

Sonya laughed. "That's the best medicine I've had all week. Sure, come on over and bring the soup."

When Walid arrived with the brown paper bag containing the two quarts of soup, Sonya greeted him at her front door wearing a thick bathrobe, flannel pajamas, and a baseball cap. "Pretty sexy, huh?" she quipped.

"Oh yeah," he agreed with a smile.

Walid removed the two quarts of soup from a brown paper bag while Sonya placed bowls and spoons on the table. She poured out generous portions in each bowl, releasing a cloud of warm, mouthwatering, chicken-y goodness. The two friends sat down and devoured their soup as if it were the ultimate delicacy and in short supply.

Between spoonful, Walid asked, "Why do Jews refer to chicken noodle soup as Jewish penicillin?"

Sonya smiled. "Well, a long-time tradition has been to offer chicken soup to the sick. It's light and it goes down easy. It was something even old-fashioned kitchens could turn out…a gift from the heart. Years ago folks thought it had medicinal value. Now, some scientific studies have said that's true. But even if it's short on science and long on tradition, when you're sick it's warm and comforting, and it does seem to make you feel better."

The two friends sat at the table and talked about school, their curriculum objectives, and future goals. Then, following a brief pause, the conversation turned to a different topic—family.

"Tell me more about your father," Walid said.

Sonya responded thoughtfully. "My father is kind and loving. He's been strict but fair in teaching Nadev and me a traditional value system. He sets rules and expects us to follow them but he's never been unreasonable or non-negotiable. When my mother died, he had to make some difficult adjustments in his daily life, and I have always admired him for how he made those changes."

"What sort of adjustments?"

"Well, working for the Israeli government, he was frequently called away from home at odd times, sometimes for long periods, and into situations no one could discuss. He may have been out of the country on missions. Who knows? He never talked about it and neither did we. After my mother died, my Dad coped by throwing himself even more into his work. He'd make sure we had money, but he'd go off and we'd be home alone."

"Sounds like some kind of secret service. Hey, was your father in the Mossad?"

"What! Why would you ask such a thing?" Sonya asked him coldly. "I told you we never discussed his work."

"Look, I'm sorry if I said anything to upset you. I just wondered if your life back there was anything like mine."

"Well, was it?"

Walid went on to discuss his own childhood years in Cairo and his middle-class family. Both parents worked hard to provide the essentials and more for their son in the hope his future would be easier than theirs. Education was recognized early on as Walid's ticket to an improved future. Wherever and whenever possible, Walid's parents tried to provide better educational opportunities so he could climb the ladder of success. Walid had done well in school and shown a strong interest in the field of science, especially physics. It was this affinity for physics and an engineering science background that helped him win a scholarship to the University of Chicago.

Walid continued, "My mother is the sweetest woman on this earth. She lives and breathes for her family and would do anything to improve my life. My father is, shall I say, the disciplinarian of the family. He's a good man, mostly, but he has a temper and sometimes he gets angry with me for no reason. If money was tight or the roof of our house began to leak, I was his target." He paused. "I respect my father but we aren't close like I am with my mother. When I left Egypt to come to the States, my mother wished me the best. She prayed for my good health, success at school, and happiness in life. My father said good-bye, shook my hand, and told me to send some money once I got a job. So I guess our families are different."

Their long talk wore on Sonya. She finally told Walid she was going to try to sleep for a while. She thanked him once again for the soup and friendly conversation. He assured her he would check up on her condition the following day. As he left and closed the door, he could hear the double bolt security lock click behind him. Sonya was a sensible girl. Walid whistled as he walked away, feeling fortunate to have made such a close friend.

Walid looked forward to meeting Nadev who was scheduled to arrive in about three weeks. Sonya's brother seemed like such a great guy. The only perplexing thing was why there was a strained relationship between Nadev and his father. Walid surmised that Sonya's father was a bad ass kind of guy. That would explain some of it. Anyway, the love and admiration Sonya felt for her father led Walid to believe he was probably a good man.

As Walid was walking toward his apartment on the north end of the campus, he heard his name shouted out from across the street. He turned to find Denise jogging towards him. Half out of breath, she said, "So, I have tickets to the play at the campus theatre for tonight at eight. Want to go with me?"

"What's playing?"

"Anne Frank. You know, the story of that German girl who…."

"I know who Anne Frank was. I'll pass on the play. Thanks anyway."

"It's a great play, Walid. Come on, we'll have a good time."

"I'm sure we would. That play has been done a hundred different times and the ending is always the same."

"Okay, have it your way, but remember, the next time you beg me to attend a fundraiser for Egyptian refugees, I may be busy."

Walid recognized Denise's version of humor and forced a sort of half-grin to show he was not offended. In truth, Walid often had the feeling that American society in general overemphasized the plights of the Jewish, African American, and Hispanic cultures while ignoring other less currently popular groups of people. Practically every campus in America had organizational support for the Jews, respect for their holidays, and frequent references to their cultures not to mention specific fundraising activities. And yet, who was paying attention to the Middle Eastern refugee problems, the Egyptian declining economy, not to mention the basic mistreatment and abuse of his Arabic neighbors? He could never completely erase those inbred concerns. Walid Kassab was not stupid. He had experienced many of the political and religious injustices first hand and he was not in the mood for another Anne Frank reminder of how badly the Jewish people were treated.

Chapter 8

At O'Hare Airport, Sonya sat alone at the Delta baggage claim area awaiting the arrival of her brother. She had checked earlier on the arrival time for Flight 207 from Tel Aviv to New York with a final arrival at Chicago O'Hare. There were no scheduled delays and the 4:35 p.m. ETA was still posted. Sonya was excited to see Nadev and couldn't believe they would have two weeks together to enjoy themselves. Attending class and studying wouldn't pull her away for too long. As an academically sound student she could afford some flexibility in her schedule. She couldn't wait to hear about what was going on in her brother's life. Nadev, handsome and bright, tended to be introverted. He preferred small intimate groups to large and loud party gatherings. He enjoyed listening to the opinions of others and aside from politics, often needed coaxing before expressing his own views. Nadev was a complex individual, and in many ways, a mystery of sorts to those around him. Sonya accepted his idiosyncrasies and adored him.

The loudspeaker system announced the arrival of the Delta flight from New York. A thrill of excitement energized her and lit her face with expectation. The next thirty minutes dragged until arriving passengers entered the baggage claim area. She looked past them until Nadev, wearing his blue baseball cap and backpack, appeared. He looked great!

"Nadev! Over here!" She waved her hand in the air.

They ran towards each other and embraced, a brother and sister who had been apart for too long. Sonya stood back and took a careful look at her Israeli brother. He was a slimmer version of his father, and not quite as tall. His bronzed skin glowed beneath his mop of black hair.

"God, Nadev." Sonya said. "You're gorgeous!"

"Thanks, Sis," he replied. "You look good, too. Are you seeing somebody, playing the field, or just practicing an immoral lifestyle?"

Sonya laughed as she usually did at her brother's remarks about her social life. "I am alone, socially active, involved in my school studies, and still waiting for my prince to arrive. Now, what about you? Are you still spreading your passion around Israel or have you settled down with one special lady?"

"My dear sister, I see you haven't changed much now that you're living in America. To answer your way too personal questions that only you would ask, I am not attached to any particular lady. I am however, socially quite active and as for the immoral lifestyle, I will hold back my comments."

"Tell me, Nadev. Are things any better between you and Dad?"

"Not really. Anything I say, the man climbs all over me. He lives, eats, and breathes that political bull crap he was taught. Well, our dad is the granddaddy of Israeli bullshit and he and I are rarely on the same plate."

Sonya's smile turned to a partial frown. "You two need to turn down your ideological rhetoric. Dad lives for Israel and strongly believes its security and survival depend largely on how well the peacekeeping functions work. You see the world through different eyes. I hope that one day, both of you will see life the same way and see each other in a brighter light. That will be a happy day for all of us!"

Nadev looked at Sonya and clapped his hands as if he were applauding a performing musician. "Sis," he said. "I love you and your cartoon-like viewpoint of the world. You look at a pile of shit and see flowers. You see our homeland as a place that is always right, always just, and always justified in doing whatever it needs to do. Our father is a living example of why our Arab neighbors dream of erasing Israel."

"Look, my dear brother," Sonya replied, "you're here for only two weeks and there is nothing that will alter the way I feel about you, so let's declare a truce on all your pent-up feelings for the time being and enjoy our time together."

"You're right," Nadev replied. "A great time together, we shall have."

During the 25-minute ride from the airport, Sonya talked about her friends, Denise and Walid. Sonya had arranged to take the next day off of

Day of Reckoning

school and planned to meet the two with her brother at Sid's Deli at 12:30 p.m. When they got to her off-campus apartment, they unpacked his luggage and relaxed in the small, homey living room with a cold bottle of white wine and a light supper.

"So, this delicatessen you're so big on, is it a crowded place?" Nadev asked.

Sonya laughed. "Are you kidding? The place will be wall-to-wall Jews and even a few non-Jews. It will be loud like a major sporting event and busy like an international airport. But you know what? The food will be some of the best you ever had!"

Sonya showed Nadev to the guest bedroom and pointed out the empty dresser and large closet for his use knowing he would probably prefer to live out of his suitcase. She threw him a pillow and spread a clean blanket on top of the bed sheet. Jetlagged, Nadev was ready for sleep. Sonya leaned over and kissed her brother on the cheek. "Love you, Nadev," she said.

"Love you back," Nadev answered with a return kiss.

As she left the room, Sonya smiled broadly. She wasn't going to worry about the volatile relationship between her father and brother. Life was too short to waste time extinguishing fires of anger that didn't need to exist. She only knew the happiness she felt having her brother near.

The next day, Sonya, Nadev, Denise, and Walid planted themselves at a table at Sid's Delicatessen for a hardy, cholesterol-filled lunch, and more importantly, to get to know one another. Between bites of hearty sandwiches, they talked about school curriculums, future aspirations, social activities, and individual preferences. Things were going well until the conversation turned to world politics.

"So, Walid," Nadev said, "as an Egyptian by birth, what are your feelings about the unrest and instability in the Middle East?"

"Come on guys," Denise groaned. "Those kinds of questions will lead to no good."

"She's right," Sonya agreed. "Let's leave politics to the politicians, at least for now."

Walid continued as if neither of the girls had spoken. "I am Egyptian, Nadev, just as you are Israeli. As for the Middle East unrest, it's a fucked up situation that has existed for many decades and probably will be for many to come. I suppose I know how you feel about the situation, right?"

"Wrong. I doubt very much if you actually know how I feel about the crisis over there."

Sonya interjected. "Please, Nadev, let's change the subject."

Walid looked straight at Nadev and said, "Look, you probably see Israel in terms of political action, doing everything good whether right or wrong. With my heritage and upbringing, I tend to lean towards the Arabic point of view."

Nadev replied without hesitation. "Yes, but unlike some Israeli Jews, including certain members of my family, I do not offer rubber-stamp approval for all of the actions taken by my government. I try to consider the needs of others with objective reasoning instead of blindly following ill-conceived and poorly executed political plans."

Sonya had enough. "That's it, you two," she said with a raised voice. "One more word on this topic, and Denise and I are out of here. I mean it!"

The two fellows looked at each other and smiled. Their eye contact suggested each wondered where the conversation was headed and what views would have been expressed next.

CHAPTER 9

The next days were filled with sightseeing tours of the Chicago area and social gatherings at various clubs, restaurants, and special events. As often as possible the twosome of Sonya and Nadev became a foursome, talking and laughing together, enjoying and appreciating one another's company more each day. When Sonya had to be at school, Nadev would wander off by himself and explore. Nadev and Walid were soon close friends, both having decided to avoid the topic of world politics in order to keep the peace. Denise looked at and treated both Nadev and Walid as brothers. She would joke with them, confide in them, and criticize them when the situation called for it. It was obvious to everyone how happy she was in the bosom of the lively quartet. She didn't care where anyone was from, what they believed in, or who they prayed to. If she liked someone, nothing else mattered.

It was a typical winter day in Chicago. Moderately high winds combined with a temperature in the teens made the wind chill factor drop to a single digit. Though Nadev never complained, he was having a hard time adjusting to the frigid weather conditions. He had been in the States once before during the winter season and had seen snow, but had never before been exposed to this kind of cold. He trudged along the sidewalk wearing his parka, hat, and walking boots given to him as gifts from his sister. His backpack and gloves added a bit of additional warmth to his body, and yet the cold still seeped in. Nadev made his way to Sid's Delicatessen to have lunch with Walid and Denise. Sonya was at school and could not miss a scheduled exam.

It was a special day at the deli. The restaurant had announced for that one day, 20 percent of the proceeds collected would benefit the Israeli Peace Fund. The donated funds were targeted for humanitarian issues, such as supporting and feeding Jewish refugees, supplying much needed medical supplies, and clothing.

Walid and Denise were already seated at a table when Nadev entered the restaurant. They waved and he joined them. Some small talk followed concerning school assignments, the weather, and upcoming social plans. When he had warmed up sufficiently, Nadev removed his outer gear and hung them on the back of his chair, then picked up the menu and began to examine it.

"Hmm, what are you having today?" Denise asked.

"A bowl of chicken soup, and a side of *kreplach*," Nadev said. He rose. "Sorry, I need to pee. If I don't get back fast enough, order for me."

As he moved off toward the back corner where the restrooms were located, a waitress approached. "Ready to order?" she said, pulling out her pad and pencil. "How about you?" she asked Walid.

"Turkey club and a hot tea." He watched her write it down, then got up from the table.

"Where are you going?" Sonya asked.

He pointed in the direction of the front of the deli. "Over to the cashier. I want to find out if non-Jewish refugees could be recipients of the donated funds. I'll be just a minute."

The waitress tapped her pad. "I don't have all day. What'll it be?" she said to Denise.

"I think I'll go for the chopped salad and coffee." She pointed to Nadev's place at the table, "And he'll have a bowl of chick…"

BOOM! The walls of the deli shattered from the explosion. Ear-splitting screams added to the noise as plaster, brick, Formica, and metal fragments flew like missiles in every direction. In the smoke and dust-filled aftermath screams of agony and shock came from beneath the rubble. Cries for help, some thin, some loud, mixed with moans from the seriously injured. Blood, tissue, and body parts were splattered against broken walls, fragmented tables, and debris-strewn floor of the restaurant.

In his bathroom stall, Nadev was blown through the door and hurled against the shattering glass of the mirrored wall. He was aware something heavy had hit his right side. He could hear nothing. Through the smoke and dust, he could see two broken bodies on the floor near him. And blood….blood everywhere before his eyes rolled back and he lost consciousness.

As the smoke dissipated, those who could move tried to get away from what remained of the deli. Others stayed, rummaging through the devastation looking for friends or trying to help those in need. The injured crawled and stumbled along the torn-up ground in hopes of reaching a safe place.

Other than several superficial cuts and bruises, Walid weathered the explosion better than most. He stumbled about the remains looking for Denise until he reached the table where they had all been seated a few moments ago. Splayed on the floor in front of him, his good friend, or what was left of her, lay shattered. Below the wet, curly mass of her hair, the right side of her face and head were completely gone leaving only the raw, underlying flesh. Her left leg above the knee had disappeared, and a metal leg from one of the chairs protruded from her abdomen like a spear impaling a wild animal. Walid stared at the grotesque carnage as bile rose in his throat. He turned away, vomited, and gasped until the dusty air that filled his lungs turned into paroxysms of coughing.

Emergency vehicles and supportive health services arrived on the scene in a matter of minutes. The destroyed restaurant was sectioned off with tape, barriers, and police who secured the site. Those survivors who could either walk to the outside or be assisted to the safe areas were triaged for the extent of their injuries. An area was marked off for the deceased. Body bags were taken from a supply truck and those involved with the identification process went to work. The seriously injured were strapped onto gurneys and placed into ambulances for transport to nearby hospitals.

Nadev was found lying unconscious in the blown out restroom. His right arm was missing up to the elbow and the remaining stump of tissue was bleeding profusely. A tourniquet was applied to stop his bleeding and medical personnel checked his body for additional injuries. As they further examined their patient, Nadev's eyes opened and he moved his left hand.

One of the emergency medical assistants noticed the movement. "Hurry! He's awake. Get him into a unit for immediate transport."

"What's his assessment so far?"

"A severed right arm with stabilized hemorrhage, multiple lacerations of a superficial nature, fragmentation wounds from the explosion, probable eardrum ruptures, and the possibility of internal hemorrhage."

Nadev tried to rouse himself and became increasingly aware of his pain level. Dazed and confused by the activities around him, he understood he was being transported to a hospital. Before being lifted onto the EMS unit, Nadev whispered the name "Sonya Levy" along with her cell phone number and repeated it twice. An attendant wrote the information on a little spiral pad and shoved it back in his pocket for later.

Walid sat on the back supply area of an EMS unit where he was checked over by an attendant. He suffered partial hearing loss, but could still understand the questions he was asked.

The attendant looked up from Walid's blood pressure cuff and remarked, "Got to tell you, buddy, you're one lucky fella to be alive."

"My friend, Nadev Levy…what happened to him?" Walid asked. "I was with two friends, Denise and Nadev. I found Denise, dead. But what about Nadev? Is he alright? Please, tell me about my friend."

"Try not to worry," the attendant said. "We'll find out about your friend. First, give me your name, age, and address."

Walid froze for a moment, then shook his head as if coming to his senses. "My name is Kaleet Asad, age 19," he said. "I'm a university student, and I have an Egyptian student visa."

"You got it with you?"

Walid felt in his pocket. "No."

The attendant wrote down the pertinent information on a sheet of paper attached to his clipboard. As if he were dictating the information verbally he read aloud the data. "Kaleet Asad. Egyptian student visa. Student housing at the university. "Is there a phone number where you can be reached?"

Walid gave him a false phone number, wincing as a second medical attendant applied an antiseptic solution to several of the lacerations and bandaged them with small dressings. When the two medical assistants finished with their evaluation and treatment, one of them said, "Mr. Asad, please sit still and wait a few moments. The authorities will be over here shortly to talk with you about what happened."

"What authorities?" Walid asked in what he hoped was a calm voice.

"You know, the cops that investigate these sorts of things. They'll want to know what you recall."

As the medical technician moved on to another injured survivor, he caught a glimpse of movement. Walid was making a hasty exit.

"Stop!" The attendant yelled, "Hey! Wait! You can't leave until they talk to you."

By the time the medical attendant reached a nearby police officer to report the incident, Walid had merged into the crowd of onlookers and was nowhere to be seen. People were still being assisted out of the destroyed restaurant, and in an early development, a young Egyptian male who had miraculously survived the explosion with superficial injuries had fled the scene and become a "person of interest" or suspect.

Chapter 10

As Sonya left her psychology class, her cell phone rang. She didn't recognize the caller ID. He identified himself as an EMS attendant.

"Is this Sonya Levy?" he asked.

"Yes. Is there a problem?" she asked. "Is this about my brother, Nadev? Is he okay?" Her heart pounded and her stomach clenched.

The medical attendant explained briefly about the explosion at Sid's Delicatessen. Her brother had survived and had been taken to the University Hospital for treatment. The extent of his injuries were undetermined. She could see him at the hospital emergency room.

"I'll leave right away," she replied, wiping away tears of fear and concern.

"And, miss, keep a good thought. Your brother will get excellent care."

Sonya hung up and tried to compose herself before calling her father's cell phone in Israel. As she waited for a response, she prayed he would not be on a mission where answering the call was impossible. The phone rang three times before her father answered. Sonya burst into tears and with difficulty, blurted out the news.

"Dad," she cried. "It's Nadev. He was at a restaurant and there was an explosion and he's alive, but injured. Oh, Dad, I'm going to the hospital now. They don't know how bad it is and I'm so scared!"

"Listen, Sonya," her father interrupted, "you have to calm down and be strong at a time like this. Go to the hospital. Be with your brother. He needs you. Keep your cell phone charged and with you at all times. I will stay in touch and I will be on the first available flight I can get to Chicago. As soon as I land, I'll be with you, honey, and we'll deal with this together. Now, tell me what you know about the explosion."

"I don't know anything. I was in class when it happened. Nadev was with a couple of my friends at our favorite Jewish deli. Oh, God, what if they're injured...or dead?" She began to weep again.

Explosions at restaurants inhabited largely by Jewish patrons were not a foreign topic to Alon Levy. The difference between religious and/or racial hate crimes and international acts of terror was at least, to those involved, a moot point. While Sonya talked, his trained mind was already gearing up to another level. He was most anxious to get to the States and his children as quickly as possible.

Alon wasted little time packing for the trip. He threw a few toiletries, a couple of shirts and underclothes into a military-style duffle bag. He carried a black parka. Anything more than that could easily be purchased in Chicago. Alon's only concern was the health and welfare of his children. He understood Sonya would be there for her brother, but he needed to be there too, with his son.

Sometimes it pays to know the right people. The first flight on El-Al Airlines the following morning was at 8:20 a.m. and Alon Levy was given priority flight arrangements. It arrived in New York at 4:07 p.m. and continued on to Chicago. He talked to Sonya twice during the flights for updated information on Nadev's condition. Nadev had undergone surgery to repair his missing right arm. While he was under anesthetic, they performed an exploratory procedure to locate and repair internal bleeding from his damaged right kidney. Sonya told her father that Nadev had done well and was in the critical care unit for observation.

When the final flight touched down in Chicago, Alon hurried through the airport terminal. He hailed a cab and told the driver to get him to the University Hospital as quickly as possible. The 35-minute ride by cab seemed interminable. Fatigue from the trip only served to jumble the concerns running through his mind. Finally, the cab pulled up to the emergency room entrance and Alon rushed in.

He made his way to the critical care waiting room.

"Dad!" Sonya cried, and ran toward him. She hugged her father tightly and wept from a mixture of love, fear, relief, and fatigue. Her eyes were red and swollen, and she had neither slept nor eaten since her arrival at the hospital.

Her father continued to hold her. "How is he doing? What do the doctors say?"

"His surgeon, Dr. Green, says Nadev is doing well. If he continues to recover in the next couple of days, they'll move him to another room. Now that you're here, he'd like to speak with you."

Alon stepped back and looked at his distraught, disheveled daughter. "Now listen to me carefully, honey," he said. "I want you to go home, eat something, take a nice hot shower, and a long nap. I'll stay here and take care of things. Don't argue with me, please. Do as I say. The worst is over and Nadev is healing. It's time for you to take care of yourself. Tomorrow, when you feel ready, you'll come back and relieve me. Okay?"

Sonya knew her father was right. "Okay," she replied. "Call me if anything changes or if you need anything. I love you, Dad."

"And I love you, princess. Now, go on home."

Sonya kissed him good-bye and when she left, Alon noticed the news being reported on the wall-mounted television. The commentator was talking about Sid's Delicatessen. In the two days since the explosion, the investigation had been shared by Homeland Security authorities and the FBI, who was heading up the procedures. Alon's attention was interrupted by a nurse asking if she could be of assistance. He gave his name and requested to meet with Dr. Green about his son, Nadev Levy. He asked to be taken to his son.

Alon Levy by anyone's measure had inner strength. He had seen and done things that would turn the stomachs of most people, but he was also a father, and the sight of his son lying unconscious with tubes, intravenous lines, and multiple connections to monitoring devices left him feeling sick. As he sat bedside and held his son's motionless hand, he thought back to their recent confrontations that had ended with angry feelings. If only he could have erased or undone those moments.

Dr. Green entered the room. Alon stood and shook his hand.

"Mr. Levy? I'm Dr. Green, your son's surgeon. Please, stay seated, and I'll bring you up to date."

"I'm listening."

"Your son lost his right arm in the explosion about an inch below the elbow. He lost a fair amount of blood from the injury. We were able to adequately clean up the torn tissue, stop the bleeding, and create a stump for a prosthesis—for later, you understand. He also sustained an injury to the right kidney, which resulted in a moderate internal organ hemorrhage. We identified the site—it's a contained area—and successfully repaired the damage. He received two blood transfusions to replace what he lost. I removed multiple fragmentary pieces of brick, wood, and plaster—similar to shrapnel from an explosion—from your son's body. He will probably suffer some degree of hearing loss. It's too early to assess the damage and/or the longevity of related complications. I know that this is a lot of information to hear at one time. Do you have any questions?"

Alon sensed Dr. Green's sincere empathy, professional maturity, and felt confidence in his surgical abilities. "Questions?" Alon replied. "Too many to throw out there right now. If I understand you, in time, my Nadev should be okay. Is that right, doctor?"

"Yes. Nadev is very lucky he was in another room, away from the explosion source."

"What do you mean?"

"The restroom. There was a wall that separated him from the blast."

"Has my son been conscious at all? I mean does he know about his arm?"

"He does." Dr. Green took a last look at his sleeping patient. "Well, if you have no further questions, I'll get back to work and you can visit your son in privacy. I don't know how long he'll need to be here. We'll take it one day at a time. Contact me if you need to." He handed Alon his business card.

Alon shook the doctor's hand. "Thank you for your help and for giving me back my son. I owe you big time," he said.

Alon gazed down on his son. He felt a sense of comfort as his son lay peacefully in the bed with his eyes shut. He had never felt closer to Nadev.

CHAPTER 11

Alon Levy spent his first night in Chicago curled up cat napping on a short couch in his son's hospital room. Each time a nurse entered to check on the boy's vital signs, his father would open his eyes and sit up so as not to miss any clinical change. Before dawn the following morning, Nadev opened his eyes and showed visible signs of irritation from the tubes in his nose and various parts of his body. The next time a nurse came in to check on Nadev's vital signs, she adjusted his tubes, changed the bandage over the kidney incision and replaced Nadev's catheter bag. When a doctor arrived for his rounds he asked Alon to limit his conversation, to encourage the young man to rest.

Alon acknowledged the request, and then turned to Nadev. "How ya doing, son?" he asked.

Nadev looked at his father and half smiled. He tried to speak, but couldn't articulate any meaningful sounds.

"Don't try to talk, Nadev," his father said. "It's alright. You're going to be fine. That's what counts. I'm going to step out and call your sister with an update. I'll be right back. I love you, son."

Nadev slowly closed his eyes and fell back asleep. As Alon turned down the hall, he was greeted by a man in his mid-thirties dressed in a dark suit, and an attractive woman of about the same age wearing business apparel. Alon knew immediately they were FBI or Homeland Security personnel.

"Mr. Levy?" the woman asked. Alon nodded. "It is a pleasure to meet you, sir. We understand your son is doing well. Good news, indeed. We are Federal agents on the lead investigation team dealing with this event. I'm Agent Rebecca Kurnitz and this is my partner, Agent Richard Cramden."

They shook hands and decided to have coffee in a nearby conference room. Agent Cramden closed the door for privacy.

"You know, Mr. Levy," he said, "I've been looking forward to meeting you. At the Academy, your texts on dealing with terrorism and interrogation techniques were required reading. They are well written and informative to say the least."

"Thank you. I appreciate your comments. Now, I'd like to know what happened at that restaurant."

"In a moment," interjected Agent Kurnitz. "There is something we must discuss and agree upon."

Alon nodded. "Go on."

"Washington recognizes your abilities. We could use your expert assistance in the investigation of this case. However, in order to include you as a consultant, you would first have to agree to certain stipulations."

Alon could feel his irritation rise. "Agent Kurnitz," he said, "we both have a lot of things to do this morning, so let's drop the bullshit and say what is really going on here."

Cramden spoke up. "In short, Mr. Levy, we could utilize your help. but cannot use you in any capacity other than as a consultant. You would have to assure us of your agreement before we could share what information we have."

"And what exactly constitutes a consulting role?"

"Essentially," Kurnitz said, "you will review evidence and accumulated data and advise us as to how you would proceed. You will not participate routinely on field investigations, active pursuits, or resultant arrests. Furthermore, we may choose to follow or ignore your advice depending on our conclusions at the time. After all, those of us involved in this case are also well trained and have good field experience."

"Oh? Then tell me Agents Cramden and Kurnitz, if your expertise is so phenomenal, and I am sure it is, why use me at all?"

Kurnitz replied. "You have a certain reputation in the civil law enforcement arena. We know if we don't include you in our investigation process, you'll probably start doing some fishing around yourself and we can't have that. Your operational procedures in Israel are different from our system here."

"I understand. I have no jurisdiction here in Chicago. I will agree to reviewing data, hearing pertinent evidence, and making suggestions as to how one might proceed. Hopefully, my information will prove beneficial. If not, you can choose to follow whatever course you want. I will not participate in your field activities nor any combined pursuit or arresting process. However, my son Nadev had his right arm blown off and nearly died in what appears to be a terrorist explosion in a Chicago restaurant. The person or persons who perpetrated that cowardly act affected my family. That means I'm already involved. So, I will operate within the law. But you can be sure that I will not sit around waiting for your written reports to arrive."

"Mr. Levy, thank you. We have asked for your assistance and you have agreed to give it. But it is essential that you stay out of our way when it comes to the actual investigation procedures. If necessary sir, we can apply pressure to stop you."

Alon looked directly at Agent Kurnitz, and replied in a low-pitched monotone, "I don't give a shit which organization you're with or what rules you play by. I'll tell you one thing though, don't ever threaten me. And if you even think about applying pressure, you'll get into waters you won't know how to get out of. I promise you, this is one Israeli agent you won't want to piss off. Now, do we understand one another? And how do we proceed, if at all?"

Cramden answered, "We'll try the cooperation route for a while and see how it works. Here is a card with clearance to our department at the office. Show it to the person at the main desk and you'll be buzzed through the entrance door. It's now 10:00 a.m. Let's meet and review the initial evidence and data at about 2:00 p.m. Does that work for you?"

"Yes, two o'clock it is. But if I'm needed at the hospital, I'll call you to reschedule." He offered a hand to Cramden, who shook it, then turned and made the same gesture to Kurnitz who merely said good-bye, turned and walked away.

Alon Levy left the hospital and took a cab to a nearby restaurant for lunch. He called Sonya and told her to meet him there. They would eat and relax for an hour and then go back to the hospital. When she arrived, he stood up and greeted his daughter with a hug and kiss. Alon informed Sonya of Nadev's improved condition, as well as his discussion with the two FBI agents. The casualty list from the explosion had not been released yet to the public and wouldn't be until positive identifications were complete and the families had been notified. Sonya was worried sick since she hadn't heard from her friends, Walid and Denise. She knew the three of them were meeting for lunch at the deli, and the night before had told Nadev she could not be there because of her school exam. Alon assured her that as soon as possible, he would find out about her friends.

Without thinking about specifics, Alon, in his naturally curious and highly investigative manner questioned Sonya. "Tell me about Sid's Delicatessen."

"What do you mean Dad?"

"You know, how busy does it get at lunchtime? What is the customer base like? Age, socio-economic, and religious affiliations. That kind of thing."

"Well," she said, "the place is packed with people at lunchtime. You have to wait at least fifteen to twenty minutes to get a table. The customers are a general mix between university types, business people on lunch breaks and folks who live around here. Plenty of ethnic and age mix. As you'd expect, dress is pretty casual. Religious affiliations? It does seem to be a magnet for the Jewish community. I suppose a majority of its customers are Jewish."

"And is there anything you can think of that would make the place a target?"

Sonya thought a moment. "Maybe. That day, the deli was running a fundraising event. Twenty percent of the day's proceeds were to be donated to an Israeli fund. Dad, what do you think it all means?"

"I don't know, honey. Not yet anyway." The food came and the two ate lightly. At the end of the meal, Alon told Sonya he needed to attend a meeting with the FBI agents at 2:00 p.m. "Go to the hospital and stay with Nadev. When the meeting's over, I'll get a cab and join you."

"Don't forget, Dad," Sonya said. "See if you can find out about my friends Denise Baker and Walid Kassab."

Chapter 12

The FBI headquarters in downtown Chicago was a six-story grey brick building. The main lobby resembled a federal county courthouse with its marble floors, tall glass windows, and centralized walkways. An elaborate metal detection unit was planted just inside the entryway, and a large, imprinted insignia of the Federal Bureau of Investigation, set in tile on the floor in the center of the main lobby announced the building's purpose. Alon had been to the FBI center in Washington, D.C. about three years ago as a guest speaker and trainer at a seminar dealing with international and homeland terrorism.

Levy showed his identification card to an armed guard seated at the side of the metal detector. Alon walked slowly through the device with his arms raised. On the other side of it he was patted down and escorted by one of the guards through a door to the departmental offices in the back. A short ride to the third floor on the elevator, a turn to the right, and the guard pointed to the desired investigation office. Alon gave his name to the receptionist and noted his scheduled appointment with agents Kurnitz and Cramden. He was buzzed through the security door and greeted by Agent Cramden.

"How's your son doing, Mr. Levy?" Cramden asked.

"Much better, I believe. Thanks for asking."

The two men entered a private office and sat down at a conference table. Almost at the same moment, Agent Kurnitz entered the room. "Good afternoon, Mr. Levy," she said. "How are things on the home front? I mean your son's condition, your daughter, and you, too. How is everyone coping?"

"I think everything will be alright. Thanks for your concern," Alon said.

Day of Reckoning 45

"So," Agent Kurnitz said, "let's get to work. I'll start by giving a brief up-to-date status report."

Alon sat quietly and prepared to take notes on the small memo pad he removed from the breast pocket of his jacket.

"The bomb was detonated at 12:07 p.m. on Saturday during the lunchtime rush at Sid's Delicatessen. The casualties include eleven dead, four in critical condition, and thirteen others with non-life threatening injuries who were either treated and released or admitted for observation. The restaurant itself was completely destroyed in addition to moderate structural damage to the adjacent businesses on either side of the explosion site."

Alon asked, "Is anything known about the explosion itself from forensic studies?"

Agent Cramden grabbed a report from the table and handed it to Alon while talking about its findings. It showed that the explosive source was military grade C4 plastic and the probable detonation mechanism was either a timer, as yet undiscovered, or a cell phone. Further examination of the destructive force and direction indicated the position of the bomb to be most likely in the restaurant's mid-section.

"That's where the worst destruction and highest death count would have come from, with lesser injuries on the outer periphery. Right?"

"We don't have a diagram yet showing positions of the dead and injured in situ. Not sure what the holdup is for that," Cramden answered.

"There is one other item worth mentioning," Agent Kurnitz said.

"And what is that?" asked Alon.

"One of the survivors who sustained minor injuries, and was attended to at one of the EMS units, was an Egyptian, nineteen-year-old engineering student at the University of Chicago. He was told to wait until the investigators questioned him. Several moments later, the attendant noticed him running away from the emergency unit into the crowd of onlookers. He was pursued but not found. The name he gave us was traced and found to be non-existent. That is to say, there is no such student at the university with that name. The phone number he gave was also fictitious."

Alon Levy heard the news with a stoic face. "Why am I not surprised?" he said.

"Meaning?"

"Well, you have a young Egyptian man in the same location as the bomb. He walks out of the explosion with only minor wounds and runs when told to stay for questioning. He gives you a phony name and phone number and doesn't exist as a student according to the University sources. Need I say more?"

"Here's the thing," Agent Kurnitz said, "In the United States, we are legally refrained from making judgments based on profiling. That's what you're doing. He's Egyptian, so naturally, you think he's our guy. Certainly that is possible but it's not a given."

Alon's face turned crimson red with anger. "First of all, Agent Kurnitz," he said, "profiling is a way of life in Israel. We're a small country surrounded by a lot of people who would love to see us gone. So yes, we profile as a matter of survival and as a factor of probability. Now, you, on the other hand, profile as well, but refuse to admit to it because of its so-called political incorrectness. It is interesting though, how since the attack in New York on 9-11, of the thirteen terror attacks against your country, eleven have been committed by radical Islamists. And you are going to stand here and tell me profiling is a terrible policy? It might be morally distasteful, but it is certainly indicated, not to mention being widely utilized."

Agent Cramden thought it wise to change the subject. "Mr. Levy, what more do you think we should be doing right now from an investigational standpoint?"

After a moment's thought Alon said, "You have to start creating two grids or internal drawings of the explosion site. One grid would map out where the injured individuals were located and the extent of their injuries. That will show us a more accurate location of where the explosive device was positioned. The second grid will indicate to the best of our knowledge who was sitting where when the bomb went off. This may or may not provide useful information, but might help to support or negate some of our findings or conclusions."

"Excellent suggestion," Kurnitz said. "We should hold a follow-up session in the next couple of days." Everyone agreed.

Alon remembered Sonya's request to find out about her friends. He decided to hold back Walid's name. He wanted to check that one out on his own.

"Agent Kurnitz," he asked. "I'd appreciate it if you could you tell me about the status of a close friend of my daughter, a Denise Baker."

Kurnitz looked up the name on the casualty list. "I am sorry, but Denise was killed and her family has been notified. Please ask your daughter not to spread the news around to other students or friends out of respect for them."

"I understand, and thank you."

As the meeting broke up, Alon asked Agent Kurnitz to stay to speak to her in confidence. Agent Cramden was not offended and left the room.

"Agent Kurnitz," said Alon. "would it be okay if I call you Rebecca, and you would call me Alon?"

"Absolutely. No problem," she replied.

Alon said, "I feel you and I might have gotten off to a bad start and I'd like to begin again with a friendlier relationship. What do you think? Can we give it a try?"

"Alon, look, I'm sorry if I seemed angry or off base. It's a territorial issue. I mean, I didn't request your help on this case. We are all trained and experienced law enforcement agents. You have a well-respected reputation of being a problem solver. All of a sudden, I was told by my superiors to include you in our investigative process. I think you can see how some animosity might have crept in."

"Rebecca," Alon said, "believe me, I am not here to step on toes or otherwise interfere with your work. If you ever feel that I am overstepping my role, just tell me. But in the meantime, let's be friends and nail the bastard that did this!"

"Amen to that!" she replied.

Chapter 13

Alon memorized the maze of hallways leading to his son's hospital room. This time, as he reached the room, his heart dropped and his breathing quickened. An attendant was smoothing out fresh linens on an empty bed.

"Where is my son, Nadev Levy?" Alon asked.

"Oh, he's been transferred to room 304 on the non-critical floor," she replied. "And I think your daughter is with him."

Alon took the elevator and quickly found room 304. It was a smaller room and without all of the sophisticated high-tech medical monitoring equipment. Nadev was lying in bed with his eyes open. Sonya was sitting in a chair near the head of the bed. Joining them was Dr. Green, who had just finished applying a fresh bandage to Nadev's right arm stump. He turned when Alon entered the room.

"Nadev, Sonya, hi kids," Alon remarked. "It's good to see that you've been moved Nadev."

"Hi, Dad," Sonya replied. "Now that you're here, I'm going to step out for a few minutes to get something to drink. I'll be right back."

"How is the patient doing today, doctor?" Alon asked. "It looks like he's almost ready to go jogging."

Dr. Green said the young man's stump was healing well, any sign of internal hemorrhaging had stopped, and the injured right kidney had regained its function. Regarding the hearing loss, the doctor noted that Nadev had recovered about thirty percent of his auditory capacity and that further progress was anticipated. He excused himself to continue his rounds.

Alon bent over the bed and kissed his son on the forehead. Nadev whispered, "Good to see you, Dad."

"I was worried sick when your sister called about you being caught in an explosion. I pulled some strings and was on the next flight into New York. The doctor just gave you a pretty good report. That should make you feel better."

"Sure. I feel lucky to be alive. But my right arm...it...it's gone!"

"Don't think about it. Amazing things can be done with prosthetics these days. Thank God you're still here. Do you remember anything about the explosion?"

Nadev sighed. "I remember getting up from the table and going to the restroom. The explosion went off and brick, glass, and plaster shards were flying everywhere. That was the last thing I remember."

"Do you remember who you were sitting with at the table?"

"Yeah. I was with Denise and Walid; Sonya's friends. We've been seeing a lot of each other since I got here."

"Tell me something, Nadev. How well did you get to know Walid?"

"I guess we got to know things about each other."

"How about his political views? Did he ever talk about his feelings about Middle East politics, specifically about Israel and its Jewish population?"

"I don't know Dad," Nadev said wearily. "He was born and raised in the Middle East so his Arabic upbringing was most likely not pro-Israel."

"Is that your impression of his ideology, or did his comments support that point of view?"

"There were several times when Walid made negative comments about Israel and its political actions in the Middle East. Sonya didn't always agree with them and didn't hesitate to state her point of view."

"These comments about Walid are starting to sound like past discussions you and I have had," Alon said.

"You've got a point there, Dad," Nadev replied. His eyelids fluttered and closed as the effects of his IV pain medication took hold. He was soon asleep.

Alon stepped out into the hallway for a short break. He found a chair and sat down. Sonya turned the corner and approached with a take-out cup of coffee in her hand.

She asked her father about her friends, Denise and Walid. Alon chose his words carefully and decided for the time being to withhold the information about the possibility that Walid had fled the scene. "We're not sure, but it is believed Walid survived."

"And Denise?"

He stood up and hugged Sonya to him. "I'm so sorry, but the news about Denise was bad. She didn't make it."

The sounds of mournful crying filled the hallway. After she composed herself, Sonya asked for any details regarding the death of her friend. Alon responded by assuring her that it was probably quick and painless. She was seated, he believed, near the source of the explosion.

The two of them went back into Nadev's room for more privacy. The first issue Alon wanted to carefully explore was the nature and sequential development of Sonya's friendship with her Egyptian friend. During the next hour or so, Alon inquired about how they met, the type of relationship they had, and any past history Walid may have discussed. Alon explained away the purpose of the inquiry as useful information to assist in the search procedure. He felt that this was the wrong time to tell Sonya that Walid was a primary suspect. It was obvious Sonya and that young man had established a strong bond of friendship, and hearing accusations about his involvement would be emotionally devastating.

Sonya was too smart to be misled by her father's questioning. She had questions of her own. "Dad," she said, "For real. What's actually going on here? Why all the questions about Walid? This isn't some Mossad investigation. This is you talking to me, so tell me for God's sake. No evasions, no cover-ups. What is going on?"

Alon took a deep breath and exhaled slowly. "I didn't want to add to your grief," he said. "You want the truth? Here it is." He told Sonya about the Egyptian student who gave false personal information and then fled the scene with only minor injuries, before he could be questioned by the authorities.

Sonya's reaction was a mixture of shock and denial. Walid was her friend and she couldn't believe for a minute that he was capable of committing such an act. "Believe me," she said, "there must be some kind of explanation for Walid's actions at the bomb scene—assuming it's him. You don't know that. He is a good person, and you have to swear to me you'll keep an open mind. At least reserve your judgment until you hear his side of the story."

"Honey, I'm merely a consultant here, not the main authority. I'd be very interested to hear his story, but I've got to tell you it doesn't look good for your friend right now. Do you have any idea where he might go?"

"No."

Nadev awakened and was listening to the ongoing conversation. Alon turned his attention to his son and said, "Nadev, you heard our discussion. Do you have anything to add?"

Nadev was woozy from the drugs in his system. "Dad, I don't know Walid as well as Sonya, but I'd be surprised to know he's a suspect in such a thing."

"The authorities think he's in hiding. Where do you think he might be?"

Sonya and Nadev both shook their heads.

There was a knock on the hospital room door, and Agents Cramden and Kurnitz entered the room. After greeting Sonya and Nadev, they asked Alon if they could speak to him in the hallway.

Once outside, Cramden said, "Our investigation has turned up the name of an ex-con in the area who served seven years of a twelve-year sentence for setting off pipe bombs at shopping malls and in schoolyards. His name is Marcus Deutch and he's one of those Aryan gang members who hates blacks, Jews, and just about everybody outside of his circle of white supremacists."

Rebecca Kurnitz said, "We don't think he's our guy, but we'll check him out anyway. He likes to hang out at the Sandy Dog Bar and Grille between 11:00 a.m. and 4:00 p.m. We'll let you know what we find out after our visit this afternoon."

Alon made a mental note of it and said, "Thanks for filling me in. I look forward to hearing the results."

The agents turned and left. Alon took out a pen and pocket notebook and jotted down the names, Marcus Deutch, Sandy Dog Bar and Grille. Then he returned to his son's bedside.

"I got here in the middle of Dr. Green's visit," Alon said. "Did he mention anything important before I got here?"

Nadev brightened. "Yes, he told me the stump of my arm is healing well and I might be discharged in a day or two. Sonya can pick me up and I'll stay at her place. I'll call the airlines and postpone my return flight."

"Dr. Green showed me how to change his wound dressing," Sonya added. "I can do it."

"I'm supposed to return for a follow-up visit in one week. That's good news, isn't it, Dad?"

"Absolutely!"

Alon kissed Nadev good-bye. Before he could reach the door, Sonya turned to follow. "Dad, let me walk you to the lobby."

Once in the hallway, Sonya said, "Listen to me. I know you, and somehow you'll go on a hunting mission for Walid. Please don't hurt him. Give him a chance to explain himself. He's my good friend. I still believe in him and pray this whole thing will turn out well. Now, promise me, Dad, that you will have an open mind and give him a chance to explain!"

"I will do my best to respect your wishes," he said. "After all, I am not the police or the FBI and believe me, they are intensely searching for your friend as we speak. If by chance he contacts you, persuade him to turn himself in for his own safety." The two hugged and parted company.

Apart from the fact that Alon believed the present evidence did not look good for Walid, he was sure of one thing. He would pay a visit to Marcus Deutch. In his gut, he was convinced the ex-con had nothing to do with the delicatessen bombing, but it was his nature to cover all possible leads. He had made a mental note of the man's name and hangout. Tomorrow Alon would visit Mr. Deutch for a little conversation and what would surely be an eventful visit. Knowing that Deutch was affiliated with the Aryan sub-culture, Alon grinned at the thought of a meeting that seemed made for the movies. Israeli Jew meets Aryan Neo-Nazi at local bar. That's what the newspaper headline would read. The rest of the content and conclusion were yet to be written.

CHAPTER 14

Sonya and her father returned to Nadev's hospital room and sat together as a family. Alon asked most of the questions he had about Walid, but years of investigative training and field experience required him to revisit many of the same issues to establish consistency. It did not take long for the topic to continue, for while the Levy family had dinner together in Nadev's room, Alon's mind reeled with thoughts of the missing Egyptian.

"Sonya," he said. "Tell me again about your relationship with Walid. You know, what was he like? What were his views about Jews, Israel, and the increased violence in the Middle East?"

"Dad, we've been through all of this. Look, you know me well and I am telling you, Walid Kassab was not just a casual acquaintance. He was a close friend and that should be enough information on its own."

"I'm sorry, honey, but it isn't enough. I have to ask you these questions because I need to know everything possible about him. Now please, help me and those that suffered from this terrible incident by giving whatever information you can about Walid, even if you think it's trivial."

"If you insist. We were close friends. There was nothing romantic going on. We were just friends. He did feel that the Egyptian people, and some other Arabic countries, were singled out in a negative sense and treated unequally by the American government as opposed to America's treatment of Israel. As for Jewish people, he never expressed a negative viewpoint and in fact, was a close friend to me knowing I was an Israeli. In every sense of the word, I would state that Walid Kassab was a non-violent, politically inactive, engineering major who was working hard to maintain his university scholarship."

The two of them quietly finished their meals. Nadev had already nodded off. Finally Sonya asked, "Dad, what is your role in this whole mess?"

"What do you mean?"

"I mean, the FBI, Homeland Security, local police, they're all directly involved in the investigation and then there's you. I don't understand how you fit into this process."

"They've asked me to play a consultant's role during the investigation. I review evidence, listen to reports, and then recommend strategies for further investigation efforts."

"Uh, huh. And at this very moment, do you believe Walid Kassab is a viable suspect? Do you believe in your heart he did this ghastly thing?"

Alon drummed his fingers while considering his response. He never wanted to lie to his daughter. However, an honest answer could bring unwanted results. If Walid contacted Sonya, she would tell him not to speak to her father. He chose his words carefully. "Although there is strong evidence to suggest he did commit the act, I have a lot of faith in your choice of friends and your gut feelings about him. I'm on the fence. I need to hear his explanation. I'll try to remain open minded, as you said. I'll try."

Chapter 15

The Sandy Dog Bar and Grille was a seedy looking establishment in a seedy part of town with equally seedy looking patrons. Alon Levy got out of the cab and asked the driver to wait. He grunted at the ironic thought of returning to the hospital after the upcoming visit. His intention was to spend several hours with his son, not to receive medical care as a result of the Sandy Dog visit. Alon wanted to meet and talk with Marcus Deutch and draw his own conclusions about the man's possible involvement. He had already reviewed the field report by the FBI that indicated Deutch, a repulsive character, was not considered a primary suspect. Alon knew his reception would not be pleasant. His goal was to form a general impression of Deutch's character before writing him off as a suspect. Even though it appeared the Egyptian kid was the culprit, good police work involved checking out other possible candidates.

As Alon entered the bar, his eyes had to adjust to the dimly lit room reeking of the smoke of unfiltered cigarettes and more than a whiff of marijuana. As he looked around, he instinctively noted the number of patrons who looked like potential trouble, where they sat, and the location of all exits. In addition, there was a bartender who looked like a motorcycle gang member, and a waitress who was busy wiping table tops. An older gentleman sat by himself with a full bottle of beer and two empties. He seemed harmless, but the remaining two seated at a table near the front window were a different story. It was 12:30 p.m. and Alon assumed that Deutch, his man of interest, was one of them. Speaking loudly with his strong Israeli accent, he asked the bartender where he should sit to get a burger and a beer.

One of the two men seated at the table spoke up. "Where's that accent from fella?"

"I'm from Israel," Alon replied.

"Ain't that Jew land?" the guy asked.

"Yes, and you could say that in a different way."

"Don't really matter how the fuck you take it, Mister. All you need to know is this...we don't serve Jews, so get the fuck outta here before I get pissed off just lookin' at you."

"It's a good thing you don't serve Jews here because I'd rather just have a hamburger. I'm looking for a Mr. Marcus Deutch and I've got a funny feeling that's you. Am I right?"

"What makes you think I'm Deutch?"

"Because the FBI agents I spoke to said he was a stupid motherfucker who was covered with dumbass tattoos to help him imitate a would-be Nazi. They also said he was an ex-con who served seven years of a twelve-year sentence for blowing up pipe bombs at the local malls and schoolyards. And they said this guy Deutch was a real asshole who had the mind of a chicken and the balls of a miniature dog. Now, you wouldn't be Marcus Deutch by any chance, would you?"

Alon knew the response to those remarks was going to be physical and quick. He also knew the guy was Marcus Deutch from photographs shown to him by the government agents.

The two men rose from the table and ambled towards Alon. Deutch studied Alon during his approach, sizing him up. In a low, guttural tone he said, "Mister, you're gonna be one sorry Jew boy for walking into this bar. And one lucky piece of shit if you can crawl out of here when I'm done fuckin' you up."

Alon watched the other man, who hadn't said a word, creep to the side. The man held a half-filled bottle of beer in his hand. Alon felt no fear, only concern as to how badly injured he would leave these two morons.

Deutch swung first, a right fist aimed at Alon's jaw. Alon easily sidestepped the blow and with an open hand, slapped his attacker firmly on the cheek. The slap stung, turned the skin a dark pink, and humiliated Deutch, whose face burned. His partner cracked the beer bottle against the edge of a table leaving him with a jagged glass weapon he held by the bottle neck. As he got closer to Alon, he made a sudden lunge toward Alon's mid-section. Alon, in a lightning fast move, deflected the man's arm with the outside edge of his left arm, and simultaneously threw a hard fist straight into the bridge of the guy's nose. The cartilage in the man's nose made an audible *crack*, leaving his nostrils deviated to one side and gushing blood. Covering his nose, his would-be attacker dropped to the ground and wailed in agony as a steady flow of blood ran down his face through his fingers and onto the front of his T-shirt.

Alon's moves did not dissuade Deutch, who failed to register the potential effect of the mismatch. He had no idea Alon Levy was one of the best hand-to-hand combat training specialists, not that it would have mattered. Deutch, who had taken a step back, lunged forward and threw a left, grazing Alon on the side of his mouth. Blood trickled from his lip. Alon responded with a straight leg kick to Deutch's knee cap, causing the leg to buckle. Alon supposed he had shattered Deutch's patella, the grand finale of the short, definitive confrontation. Marcus Deutch rolled on the ground hugging his injured knee with both hands. "*Fuck! Fucking asshole!*" he cried. His buddy crawled away and settled beneath a table.

Alon bent down and grabbed the metal swastika hanging from Deutch's pierced ear. "Now listen to me very carefully," Alon said. "I'm going to ask you a question and you'll give me an honest answer. Understand, my Aryan friend?"

"Go fuck yourself, Jew boy!" Deutch replied in obvious pain. He took a feeble swipe at Alon.

"Wrong answer, Marcus." Alon ripped the metal earring through the lobe.

"*Aaah!* Fuck you!" Marcus yelled and cupped his hand over his bleeding ear.

"Let's try again Marcus and see if you can't do a little better. Here's my question, "Did you or anyone you know have anything to do with the explosion at the delicatessen?"

"No, man," Deutch sputtered. "I swear…, I had no fucking thing to do with that. Now, leave me alone. I don't know anything."

Alon smirked at the damaged man before him. "You know something, Marcus?" he said. "I hear you used to set off little explosions at schoolyards and shopping malls. If I ever hear that you do, I'm going to come back and do some serious shit to your body. Do you follow me? I hope you do because this here Jew boy is not lying."

Deutch's body trembled as he stared up at his aggressor. He said nothing. Alon turned to leave the bar and then remembered what was in his hand. He walked back to Deutch lying on the floor still holding his knee, and dropped the swastika at his feet. Alon looked at the pathetic symbol of Aryan human supremacy on the ground and said, "Marcus, make sure you wear your Nazi toy to your next meeting and remember what a tough guy you were today."

Alon walked over to the bar, pulled out a hundred dollar bill and held it in the front of the bartender. "For the video surveillance tape." Without a word, the bartender retrieved the item and stashed the hundred in his back pocket. Alon knew his kind. Money was money and a hundred dollars would buy silence.

As Alon turned to leave, the bartender asked out loud, "Say mister, ya want a sandwich to go?"

Alon smiled and kept walking. He stepped out of the Sandy Dog Bar and Grille into the brightness of day. The cabbie had parked across the street and did a u-turn. Alon got in. "I'll go back to the University Hospital now."

"All set buddy?" replied the cab driver. "Forgive me for asking, but isn't that a strange place to have lunch?"

Alon smiled and said, "The food might be dangerous, but the patrons are pretty tame!"

On the way back to the hospital, Alon pondered the available investigative data. He was sure Marcus Deutch and his buddies had nothing to do with the explosion. The purpose of his trip had been confirmed, to validate his preconceived ideas. He fully expected to hear from the FBI agents in the very near future about the Sandy Dog incident. Alon's explanation? Self-defense. After all, he was careful not to throw the first punch...just the last one.

Chapter 16

Alon sat at the kitchen table at Sonya's apartment searching the Internet for detonation devices for hand-carried bombs. A knock on the front door roused him from his work. It was Rebecca Kurnitz, who greeted him in a friendly, business-like manner. She noted the computer, spread-out papers, and heavily notated yellow legal pad spread out on the table.

"Alon," she said, "you need to refocus your thoughts. Back off. Don't let it consume you."

"I appreciate your suggestions, but this is what I do," he replied. "Someday, no doubt, I'll come back here and spend my time enjoying the wonderful sights of Chicago. For now, my thoughts and efforts are better spent trying to learn more about the details of this travesty."

Rebecca had been prepared to address Alon's over-involvement in the case. Hearing that he was only conducting a fact-finding mission, as opposed to trying to solve the crime, eased her mind. She felt more secure that he knew his place as a consultant and not as an active participant in the investigative process. It made her feel like less of a combatant in his presence.

She smiled. "I understand. Look, can we get ourselves into a friendlier working relationship? After all, we're both on the same side."

Alon answered with an affirmative nod. "Yes, that would be fine."

"Where are your children?" she asked.

"Nadev is sleeping in the extra room and Sonya will be home from school soon. Why did you come to see me?"

"It's about my department director, William Jenkins. He's a Bureau Chief. I'm sure you know the type—extremely efficient, well intentioned."

"So?"

"He believes you're getting in too deep. He wants to reduce your involvement."

"What specifically bothers him?"

"He's upset that you're withholding information from our investigative procedures while at the same time expecting us to share all of our findings. In order to continue working together as we have been doing, he insists on more cooperation from you...uh, more cooperation from both our sides."

"What exactly have I withheld, Rebecca?" Alon asked.

"In our recent discussions with your children, it seems obvious their Egyptian friend, Walid Kassab, was the same person who gave false information about his identity and fled the scene. Now, honestly Alon, are you telling us you never knew anything about this kid? Why didn't you mention it?"

"Actually, Rebecca, I questioned both Sonya and Nadev about Kassab's attitudes, politics, and possible involvement. I wasn't withholding information as much as I was trying to accumulate additional evidence. I apologize for not sharing the information sooner. It won't happen again."

Alon had no sooner finished his reply when the front door opened and Sonya came in. She threw her backpack filled with textbooks, notebooks, and other assorted items onto the sofa, kissed her father and gave a friendly greeting to agent Kurnitz. "How is Nadev doing, Dad?" she asked.

"Holding his own and seems to be getting stronger with each day," he said. "He sleeps a lot, and that's to be expected. It's partly the painkillers he's taking."

Sonya turned to Rebecca. "Say, I'm going to make some spaghetti, salad, and garlic bread for dinner. Plenty of food, mediocre cook, but excellent company. How about if you stay for dinner? And don't say 'no' because my feelings will be hurt beyond repair."

Rebecca glanced at Alon for a sign of encouragement. He nodded his head and commented that they would enjoy her company for dinner.

The dinner went well with the table conversation centered around Sonya's school, her friends and the service they attended for Denise the day before, the FBI as a career choice for Rebecca, and the many attractions of Chicago. Alon was good company, but on the quiet side. Several times, he excused himself to check in on the sleeping Nadev and any apparent change in his condition. Rebecca joined Sonya in the kitchen after dinner to clean dishes and for private social time. The two of them talked about how close Alon and Sonya were and how distant the relationship was between Alon and his son, Nadev. Sonya explained how Nadev had harbored deep seated animosity for his father, and how things worsened after her mother's death about three years ago. Alon took it hard, dealing with his own depression and new responsibilities as a single parent. Sonya explained how her father became more deeply engrossed in his work to deal with his depressive moods. Working kept his depression at bay, but it meant less quality time with his children who needed him to help deal with their loss. Sonya seemed to adapt to her father's occupational commitments, Nadev did not. His resentment of his father's work, political ideologies, and parenting attitudes festered, and left Nadev with bitter feelings towards his father.

Not wanting to dominate the conversation, Sonya asked about Rebecca's situation in life. Rebecca said she was 38 years old, a graduate attorney who had decided on law enforcement for a career. She worked hard, and eleven years earlier had graduated with high honors as an FBI agent. She married a Chicago police officer who turned out to have a serious drinking problem. Their relationship went from bad to worse and ended in divorce after three years. They had no children.

"Is your father still depressed?" Rebecca asked.

"I don't think so," Sonya said. "He still misses my mother and sometimes talks about her, especially at holiday times, but he's moved on with his life. I want more than anything for him to meet a nice woman and enjoy himself more. He really deserves it."

The kitchen door swung open as Alon walked in with an empty wine glass. "You two have been talking up a storm in here. And Rebecca," he said, gesturing at her half-empty glass, "if you're leaving your wine because of work tomorrow, I'll drink it for you."

"Go right ahead," she said. "I do have to go. Thank you both for having me to dinner. You can't imagine how pleasant it is to enjoy a delicious home-cooked meal. Alon, you have a lovely daughter." Arms outstretched, she hugged Sonya and then Alon.

When she had left the apartment Sonya put her arm around her father's shoulder and said, "Dad, I really like her."

Chapter 17

Dinner

Alon had been in Chicago for six days. After arising from his bed on the made-up sofa, he split his time between assisting his son with his physical therapy sessions and reviewing the available evidence from the restaurant explosion. So far, there had been no progress in the search for Walid and no other viable suspects were being considered.

In the early afternoon the quiet of the apartment living room was interrupted by the phone. Sonya answered. She handed the cell to Alon. "It's Rebecca."

Alon smiled. "Hello, Rebecca."

"Hi, Alon," she said cheerfully. "By the way, my friends call me Becky. You can, too."

"Alright, Becky. What's up?"

"There's something I want to go over with you, and I figured since we both have to eat, I was wondering if we could meet for a bite of dinner and talk."

"Great idea. You choose the restaurant and tell me what time."

"Luigi's on the Near North Side at 7:00 p.m. I'll pick you up since you don't know the city. How does that sound?"

"Sounds good," Alon replied. "I'll look forward to it."

The rest of the day Alon decided to take a break He played cards with his children, persuaded Nadev to do his prescribed exercises to strengthen his arm, and shared a heated discussion with his son over world politics. Upon hearing about his dinner date that night, both Sonya and Nadev teased their father about his social life and dating in general.

They wanted their father to be happy and more socially active but didn't miss a beat in using humor to criticize his life style.

Sonya, with a smile and a twinkle in her eye, warned her father to be careful and to remember that being "safe" meant using a condom.

Alon blushed. "Thank you for your concern," he said. "Remember, this is just a dinner, not a love affair. Oh, and Sonya, if I should ever need advice about the use of condoms, you would be the last person in the world I'd ask." The three had a good laugh.

At seven that evening Alon spotted Rebecca Kurnitz's car from the front window of the apartment, and went downstairs to greet her. Once they were on their way to Luigi's, Alon asked, "So, what was it you wanted to go over with me?"

"Some disturbing news came across my desk this morning," she said. "I'm sure you weren't involved. However, I have to do my job. I need to ask you something."

"Ask."

"Two Aryan group members claim you came into their hangout, The Sand Dog Bar and Grille, and harmed them. One was the man we told you about, Marcus Deutch. He was admitted to the University Hospital, and treated for a cracked knee cap and torn ear lobe. The other man was treated for a broken nose. Do you have something to tell me?"

"I did it. What did you expect me to say?"

"Alon, my God! You cannot do whatever you do at home. This is not Israel and you are not James Bond with a license to hurt others. You could easily be arrested and tried for doing what you did. Do you understand?"

"Calm down, Becky. First of all, I went in that hellhole of a bar to ask that dickhead, excuse me, Deutch, a few questions. The next thing I know, he and his Aryan brother were attacking me. Your guy Deutch threw the first punch. From then on, I just got lucky and defended myself."

"Lucky my ass," she replied. "A Mossad combat legend against those two tattooed losers would be one helluva mismatch and you know it! Do you have any proof or eye witnesses that it was self-defense?"

"As a matter of fact, I do. I gave the bartender a hundred bucks for the video surveillance tape and it will more than validate my story. Now, could we please drop this topic and go for that wonderful Italian dinner?"

"God... you're impossible," she said. "By the way, get me that tape tomorrow, and please, Alon, stay out of those places and don't start any other confrontations."

"Gotcha, Becky. Now, let's eat."

The ambience at Luigi's was Roman with the scents of Italian cuisine, photographs of the old country, and the kitchen staff yelling out Italian phrases. The food was delicious. It was easy and comfortable to make small talk. Midway through the meal, when they were both flush with good food and warmed by the ambiance, Rebecca turned serious. She placed her hand on Alon's arm. "Tell me about yourself," she said. "I'd like to know more about you than what's on those basic profile cards."

"What would you like to know?"

"Oh, for instance, how and when did you join the Mossad, and why that particular branch of law enforcement?"

"Each country," Alon began, "has its elite police force. In your country, it's probably the FBI and in ours, it's the Mossad. Due to Israel's geography and circumstances, our training is largely targeted on international terrorism. In the U.S., your primary objective is frequently centered on the investigation and apprehension of federal criminals. Ours is to ensure the existence and survival of our nation as an independent democracy. I believe in the existence of the state of Israel and I pledged my life to ensure the security of its borders."

Rebecca nodded. "I understand. How did you first get involved working with the Mossad?"

"When I was in my late teens and early twenties, I served four years in the Israeli army. I'm sure you know it's mandatory for both our young men and women to serve in the armed forces. Well, during my period of service, it became clear I had certain talents or skills that added value to my participation."

"Like what?"

"Like ones we probably should avoid talking about," Alon replied. "I was approached by higher military authorities and offered a position in the Mossad. During the next four years, I underwent an extensive training period and when I graduated the program, I was transferred to an active field position."

"Is that the usual progression?"

"Not at all. The dropout or failure rate is high and in our class alone, only three out of nine successfully completed the training."

"I have some idea of your training and, like ours, know it to be vigorous and demanding. It has to be that way to turn out the best. As an agent I've often found it difficult to have a normal social life," she said. "How did you manage?"

Alon decided to reveal a small crack in his armor. He explained how he had lost his wife to cancer a few years before and had only recently returned to some semblance of a social life. "I'm so often traveling and involved with the military, I can barely manage casual dating. A serious relationship would be difficult to sustain, even if I could find someone worth the effort. He locked eyes with her. "So, now you know about me, what about you? I don't have the luxury of seeing your profile card."

Becky talked about her days at the University of Michigan where she received her undergraduate and law school education, and then being recruited at an occupational seminar into the FBI. "I spent my first few years of service in the bureau investigating health care practitioners suspected of fraudulent federal billing practices. After a while, I was transferred to the Department of National Security and that's been my target area ever since. Socially speaking, I was married for three years, no kids, but plenty of marital combat time."

"Chose the wrong guy?"

"We chose each other. And he could be very charming when he wasn't drunk. Anyway, we separated for a while and then divorced. I had my work and as a Chicago police officer, so did he. Our relationship was not heading in a good direction. His drinking became more of an issue and we mutually decided to part company."

By the time they returned to Sonya's building Becky felt much closer to Alon. She had a better understanding of who he was, his commitment to his job and way of life. When she pulled up to the curb to drop Alon off, he leaned over and kissed her on the cheek. Alon told her what a good time he had and suggested they do it again soon. Rebecca agreed. As she drove away, both she and Alon were smiling from the pleasurable thoughts of each other's company. For the first moment in a long time, Alon Levy felt the arousal of special feelings dormant since his wife's death.

CHAPTER 18

FBI Conference Meeting

The clock read 8:58. That morning fifteen agents at the FBI home office in Chicago settled in the large conference room. All the side conversations, social planning, fidgeting with papers, folders, and coffee cups would end at 9:00 a.m. sharp when the State Bureau Chief, William Jenkins, entered the room and sat down at the head of the table. As if the scene were a scripted play, Jenkins entered the doorway right on the minute and the room grew quiet. He didn't look happy—he rarely did—making it difficult to read his mood. However, William Jenkins was a man who expressed himself clearly, directly, and to the point.

"Gentlemen and ladies," he began. "the purpose of this morning's meeting is clarification. I find it hard to understand why fifteen highly trained agents cannot locate a single college student and alleged terrorist bomber in our city. I can see how this young man might elude detection for several hours or even a day or two, but you are supposed to be the finest law enforcement personnel our nation has to offer. Certainly, one or two of you must have some creative thoughts, or even a good hunch as to how we might locate and apprehend this illusive young man for questioning. So far, there is no viable information on my desk regarding this suspect other than his nationality, age, a false name, a phony address. Need I go on? Come on! It's time for your training to kick in and produce meaningful results. And that brings me to the second point of this little get-together."

His anger was increasing and his voice getting louder. He looked up and down the conference table. "Agents Kurnitz and Cramden!"

"Yes, sir," they answered in unison.

"The two of you were assigned as the lead agents on this case. So far, the results are less than impressive and I wonder if you two were the right selection. Do you hear what I'm saying? I want results and I want them yesterday! Understood?"

Kurnitz and Cramden responded as one voice. "Yes, sir, we understand."

"Alright then, the message is delivered. Work your sources, compile your data, use your investigative skills, and report your findings to your section chiefs, Agents Kurnitz and Cramden. Be careful and thorough. Find this kid!" He slammed his hand down on the table. "Meeting is over. You can return to your offices. Kurnitz, Cramden…in my office. Now!"

The two agents looked at one another and winced in anticipatory pain. They gathered their papers and issued specific assignments to selected agents, then walked to Director Jenkins's office. After a formal knock on his door, they entered and sat down in the black leather chairs facing Jenkins's desk. He looked at them and continued his critical dialog as if he had never stopped.

"Look," he said, "a bomb goes off at a Chicago delicatessen. People are killed, maimed, and massive damage results. Then, all of a sudden, we have Alon Levy, the Israeli guru on terrorism here in Chicago caring for his injured son who was caught in the blast. Now, admittedly, I signed on to enlist his consultative help in the investigation process. But I did not authorize any sort of self-motivated or vigilante activities by Levy. Now, this incident at the bar where he was supposedly defending himself is not a condoned or appreciated activity. This is Chicago, Illinois and not Tel Aviv, Israel. Inform him in no vague terms about what consultative help means and that any future altercations will result in an early return flight home. Are we clear on this matter?"

Kurnitz and Cramden nodded their heads in agreement and that was the sum total of their "conversation" with the Director. A cold silence followed their exit from his office. Agent Kurnitz thought this was probably the first meeting she had ever attended where only one person did all of the talking. The meeting was actually a wake-up call to all involved that the game plan needed some serious stepping up.

CHAPTER 19

As Alon Levy approached the conference room at the FBI center for his next briefing session with agents Kurnitz and Cramden, he started to question the value of the unproductive meetings. Nothing had happened and each session sounded like the previous one. Alon was aware of the increased level of safeguards and possible infringements on personal rights in the American justice system, and he was convinced those same protections were the frequent cause of slowed or ineffective responses to crimes. In Israel, terrorist suspects were often identified, picked up, and questioned outside of the expansive umbrella of legal protection. Complaints of human rights violations were infrequent despite that fact that police operations were not handcuffed to the same degree as their American counterparts.

The door to the conference room was already open and the two agents were seated at the table. Alon entered and sat next to Cramden.

Agent Kurnitz took the lead. "Okay, folks," she began, "let's rehash what we know, what we want to know, and where we are in this overall investigation process. We know the explosive was hand delivered, military grade C4 plastic, and probably utilized a timing device detonator. Most likely the site was selected because of its strong Jewish customer base. To date, the explosion has left us with eleven dead, twenty-three injured, of which four are still in critical care. We still have only one suspect. At the scene of the explosion, a young college-aged male student survived the blast with minor injuries. He was taken to one of the emergency trauma stations for triage evaluation. He gave a false name and address, and then fled the scene on foot when told of anticipated questioning by the authorities. He was foreign born of Middle Eastern descent. To date, we have been unable to locate this person, but are operating on the assumption that he is still in the area. From conversations with your son, Nadev, and your daughter, Sonya, it has been established that a student friend of theirs, by the name of Walid Kassab is probably the young man in flight. He is an Egyptian national. On the day of the explosion, he was at Sid's Delicatessen, seated at a table with Nadev and a young female student friend by the name of Denise Baker who unfortunately did not survive the explosion. With our accumulated evidence to date, it would appear that Kassab is our alleged terrorist."

Alon asked for a summary version of the forensic evidence accumulated thus far. He also wanted to know more about the FBI's impression that the primary motive or objective was targeting a predominately Jewish crowd since the restaurant catered to a generalized non-sectarian lunch crowd.

Agent Cramden replied. "The forensic evidence indicates the central blast point of the explosion was somewhere on the southeast section of the restaurant...about here." He pointed to an enlarged chart of the table layout. He marked a red "X" with a dry marker on the plasticized board. "Studies of the explosive remains, destruction pattern, and analyzed substance from the bomb clearly indicate that the source was military grade C4 explosive. As for the second part of your question Alon, the answer, while perhaps more subjective, we believe to be accurate. The restaurant is a Jewish delicatessen that draws its customer base from the Jewish community as well as from Jewish students and professionals at the University. In addition, on that particular day, the restaurant was donating a percentage of its collected income to a Jewish fundraising organization in support of Israel and its political activities in the Middle East. Given those facts, our belief is that this restaurant was selected for terrorism. Someone or some group was sending a message."

Agent Kurnitz turned to Alon and asked something that had been on her mind. "How sophisticated are the detonation devices in most suicide bombings? We're talking about C4 military grade stuff. Are we dealing with a home-grown product or a supplier?"

"First of all, if you don't already know it, a twelve-year-old can be taught how to assemble one of these devices. The detonator can easily be triggered by a cell phone, and the whole lethal unit can be packed in a jacket pocket. Now, considering the timing, delivery, and destruction in this case, I would bet the explosive unit was provided by an outside supplier to a suicide bomber for delivery with instructions on how to set it off and when. Usually, the bombing suspect does not walk away from the explosion, so that part is perplexing. Do any of the survivors recognize or remember anything about the Middle Eastern kid?"

"No," Rebecca said, "there were no beneficial comments made by anyone in our interviews with survivors other than the information provided by your children. No one else remembers anyone outside their own social group. It would seem to be an anonymous crowd, and once the bomb went off, everyone's memory became a blank page in a dark book."

Chapter 20

Sonya's Apartment

As the days passed, Nadev continued his physical rehabilitation, Sonya attended her University classes, and Alon grew increasingly frustrated over the failure of the authorities to locate Walid Kassab. His growing agitation was more from his restricted input rather than by the ongoing manhunt. The FBI and local authorities in conjunction with Homeland Security personnel had thoroughly searched the surrounding areas, distributed identification photos to airports, bus terminals, train stations, and turnpike exit cashiers. In addition to these measures, undercover cops were mingling at student centers and recognized hot spots where young people hung out for social activities, yet no one had the slightest idea where Kassab was, or if, when, or where he would resurface, and that drove Alon Levy crazy.

During the next few days, Alon met several times with Agents Cramden and Kurnitz. They reviewed the schematic layout of where the patrons were seated or standing when the explosion occurred. They needed answers to specific questions, but had no idea whom to ask. How was the bomb delivered? What was its method of detonation? Who supplied the military grade C4 explosive? Who planned the operation, and why Sid's Delicatessen and not some other location of greater importance? The lack of information unnerved all of them.

On a Tuesday night, Alon sat alone on the pullout couch in Sonya's apartment reviewing investigative data provided to him by the FBI. Sonya and Nadev had retired to their rooms for a good night's sleep. It was approaching midnight and Alon decided to review the remaining data in the morning prior to his scheduled meeting at the Federal Building. He

Day of Reckoning

turned off the lamp at the side of the sofa bed and lay back with his head on the soft down pillow. Within five minutes he was asleep and standing at a stone wall in Israel overlooking the Dead Sea.

Alon's training had made him a very light sleeper. Like a dog lying limp on the carpet, at any moment a faint sound would arouse the animal into a state of alertness. So it was with Alon Levy. He was asleep, yet his senses remained alert and aware of any unusual sound or motion around him. Alon opened his eyes at the sound of the front door knob turning. The apartment had no security alarm, only a dual-locking door mechanism—a push button built into the doorknob and a common chain lock with its grooved slot about six inches above the knob. Whoever was trying to enter, knew how to do it, and at this hour of the night was not an invited guest.

In silence, Alon slid off the couch to the ground and looked around for a potential weapon. He saw nothing except Sonya's set of keys on the table next to the couch. He grabbed the keys and crouched down waiting for the intruder to enter. The locks released and the front door slowly opened. A tall man with an enormous physique wearing night vision goggles stepped into the room. In the darkness, Alon saw he held a pistol with an extended silencer attached. The man stood, scanning the room from side to side. Once convinced that the room held no danger, he crept toward the two bedrooms.

Alon fisted the keys so one protruded from between his middle fingers like a dagger. Knowing that a sudden intense light source would temporarily blind a man using night vision goggles, Alon made his calculated move. He clicked on the living room lamp and threw it towards the intruder's head. Caught unaware, the startled gunman raised his arm to block the lamp. Alon moved in with cat-like stealth. He stabbed the intruder with the key, sinking its grooved stem into the man's neck until it could sink no further. At the same time, he kicked the man's gun, dislodging the weapon from his grip. The gun hit the floor, and fortunately, did not discharge.

Blood ran down the intruder's neck. He was big, strong, and must have outweighed Alon by 40 pounds. He moved to attack, but Alon threw a punch first. The intruder blocked it and delivered a vicious karate kick straight into the Israeli's mid-section, catapulting Alon back into a wall. The man raced to the gun on the floor and picked it up. Alon dove behind the couch and heard three rapid thuds as bullets hit the thick back support of the pull-out bed. It was dark in the room and the man's night vision goggles were now somewhere on the floor.

Sonya opened her door. "Dad!" she said in a panic. "Are you alright? What's happening out there?"

The intruder turned his head toward the bedroom, giving Alon a sudden but momentary opportunity. He leapt from behind the couch and flew into the intruder, targeting the gun hand. Once again, he dislodged the weapon, and turned his attention toward finishing the threat. With a grunt he drove the firm part of his palm upward onto the intruder's nose, shoving the nasal cartilage into the man's brain tissue. He would not stop his assault until he was sure the intruder was completely and permanently neutralized. He delivered a roundhouse kick to the side of the man's head, followed by a straight right punch onto his throat. A cracking sound indicated that he had hit his mark; a broken trachea, and then confirmation, hoarse gasping as a final passage of air exited the man's throat. The man crumpled backward onto the sofa and hit the floor with his massive weight. The confrontation was over, but Alon's adrenalin level was in high gear.

Alon watched the dead man a moment longer before turning toward his daughter. Sonya ran to her father and squeezed him. She was crying, shaking with fear, and pale from the sight of the bloody remains of the dead intruder.

"I already called the police," Sonya said.

Alon knew not to interfere or contaminate the crime scene and left the dead man's body on the living room carpet where it lay. "Check on Nadev," he said. "Wait in his room until the police come. And call Rebecca Kurnitz."

As Alon stood and looked down at the man, he was struck with a sudden wave of nausea and confusion. Nausea because he had ended a man's life, a deed he never took lightly, and confusion from staring at an assassin in his daughter's apartment, who appeared to be Middle Eastern. It was not the first time he had been a target, but not in recent times. Who was it and how did he know where to find him?

Voices of several men, their boots thudding, grew louder as they traversed the apartment hallway. The room seemed to vibrate as they pounded on the apartment door. "Police! Open the door!"

Alon opened it. He was well acquainted with the routine. He raised his arms in submission and began a lengthy explanation of the incident.

Sonya gave a detailed statement of what she heard and witnessed, which supported Alon's story. Nadev stood next to his sister, but could add nothing to the story. He had slept through the confrontation. As expected, Alon was taken to police headquarters with his hands cuffed behind his back. Even though his story seemed to be one of self-defense, a man was now dead and the police had to follow the standard protocol of arrest, detainment, and interrogation. It didn't surprise Alon to hear that the intruder had no identification or car to link him to an existing location or group. His gun, Alon already knew, would be a stolen or non-registered weapon, its barrel tampered to create distinctive, non-traceable markings on the bullet casings.

Alon related the incident twice and sat alone in the interrogation room until Agents Cramden and Kurnitz arrived. "Good evening, Alon," Cramden said. "I hear you've had a busy night at your daughter's apartment. Any idea what that was all about?"

"A better question, Cramden," sneered Alon, "would be, how in the hell does a Middle Eastern assassin know where I am?"

"How do you know for sure he was an assassin?" Cramden asked.

"Jesus Christ! What's your area of expertise—house crimes? When a guy breaks into your home in the middle of the night, has no identification, a 380 caliber handgun with a silencer, and is wearing night vision goggles, he's a fucking assassin!"

"Okay, okay, calm down." Cramden said.

"You just asked an interesting question," Rebecca said. "If no one knew where you were, maybe you weren't the primary target."

"What?"

"I'm saying maybe this man was sent by someone to Sonya's apartment and unluckily for him, you were on the greeting committee."

"Why would anyone send a hit man to harm my kids?"

"Let's look into that," Rebecca replied. "Meanwhile, let's move Sonya, Nadev, and you to a safe house. Better yet, the three of you can move into my house. There will be plenty of room for everyone."

"That's very kind of you. Thanks, Becky," Alon said. "Oh, and by the way, let me see the forensic data that comes back on the intruder. I'd like to know more about the guy and who may have sent him."

Agent Cramden prickled and shifted in his overcoat as he eyed Alon. "Tell me, Alon," he said, "when you encounter physical confrontations with suspects, do they ever make it to the questioning phase?"

Alon smiled, looked directly at Cramden. "Fuck you!" he said.

Chapter 21

Once the police questioning was complete and the necessary paperwork processed, Alon together with Sonya and Nadev went to Rebecca's house for the night. Sonya and Nadev each took a guest bedroom, said good night and retired for the evening. Alon sat with Rebecca at the kitchen table.

"Bet you could use a stiff drink," she said.

"I'd settle for a beer or two if you have them."

Rebecca went to her refrigerator and retrieved a cold bottle for each of them. She looked at Alon and asked, "Well, what do you make of all this?"

"I don't know what to make of it. At first, I thought for sure that gorilla was after me. Maybe someone heard or knew where I was, so they sent a hit man to take me out. Look, Becky, you know I'm no angel. I've done things certain people might resent. But the scariest thought of all is, what if I was not the target, but just someone who happened to be in the room? That scares the shit out of me because it would mean my children were the targets."

"Alon, settle down. It isn't logical that your children would be targets."

"What is logical is not always what is real. Something doesn't smell right about this whole thing."

Rebecca placed her hand gently on top of Alon's. She stroked it lightly and assured him Sonya and Nadev would be safe, and that for the time being, Sonya should not attend classes until the situation was more secure.

Alon agreed, and added, "A father's job is to protect his children. And believe me, Becky, I intend to do just that!"

That night, while everyone else was asleep, Alon, who was staying in Becky's downstairs library, punched in a number on his cell phone. A middle-aged male with an Israeli accent picked up on the other end.

"Hello," he said. "This better be good news or damn important, because my clock says it's two in the morning."

"Yosef, this is Alon Levy. I need your help on something."

"Alon? Is it really you?"

"It is, my friend."

"Where are you and what can I do for you?"

"I'm here in Chicago and what I need from you is a clean 9mm Glock with a silencer. Squeaky clean, Yosef. Non-traceable, get it?"

"No problem. Fifty rounds I assume will do the job."

"That'd be great."

"Just tell me when and where you want it."

Alon told Yosef to meet him outside of the main entrance to the University Hospital at 10 a.m. the following morning. Alon instructed Yosef to put the gun, silencer, and pre-loaded clips into a canvas bag.

Yosef was an accountant in the downtown Chicago area and had been in business for about nine years. On the surface he was an Israeli accountant living comfortably with his family. To Alon Levy, Yosef was an active member of the Israeli intelligence community who reported various bits of information to the Mossad on a periodic basis. Yosef and his two associates were also experts in electronic surveillance.

Alon told Yosef about the attacking intruder and said he needed to find out who hired him. "If I learn anything, I'll pass it along to you, Yosef."

When the conversation ended, Alon felt better about his security and that of his family. He wanted answers, and fast!

In the morning during breakfast, Alon explained to both Sonya and Nadev the necessity of staying indoors at Rebecca's house, at least for the short term. Although they agreed to cooperate, they were not happy with the request. Nadev's only question was about how soon he could return to Israel. Alon told him Dr. Green would have to clear him for travel before any arrangements could be made. On a personal level, Alon wasn't going anywhere until Walid Kassab was apprehended and questioned.

It was time for Alon to meet Yosef at the hospital. He told his kids he was going to the drug store to get some personal items. Alon borrowed

Sonya's car for the short trip. On the way, he stopped at a drugstore and picked up an assortment of shampoo and soap he didn't need, but validated his reason for leaving the house.

When Alon arrived at the entrance to the hospital, he spotted Yosef sitting on a marble step. On his right side was a dark blue canvas lunch bag. The two men sat next to each other for several moments as if they were children waiting for recess to end.

"Did you get everything I asked for?" Alon asked casually.

"Is there anything in my prior performance record that would suggest a failure to comply?" Yosef said, sounding offended.

"No, sorry." He reached for the lunch bag.

"What else can we do to help?"

"We need to locate the source of the explosive material as well as the source of the assassin. I have a feeling the two are either the same or related. Once we find a trail, surveillance will kick in until we know more about what's inside." Alon knew that while the Israeli surveillance team was activated, the FBI would already be doing the same. Interference by an international power, even though a close ally, would not be appreciated or tolerated.

Alon returned to Rebecca's home and his children. It was time for a talk about motives, objectives, and scenarios about the intruder with both Sonya and Nadev. In the past, talks like these had often accelerated into heated discussions. Nevertheless, when Alon returned to Rebecca's home and discovered she was still at work, he knew it was the right time for a family discussion.

Seated at the kitchen table, Alon and his two children looked like a charming photo portrait except for the lack of smiles. "Sonya," he said, "please put away your cell phone. Nadev, try to concentrate on what we're going to discuss." Both looked at him attentively. He turned to Sonya. "Honey, listen carefully to me. Is there anything, and I mean *anything* you could have said or done that might have resulted in someone wanting to hurt you?"

"Dad, no. Why would I be a target for some thug with a gun?"

"Let's assume for a minute that this kid, Walid, that you are friends with, turned out to be the terrorist. Was there anything he ever said to you, or you to him that would possibly have led to this?"

Once again, Sonya not only defended Walid, but emphatically denied anything that could have precipitated what had happened at the apartment. Getting her address would not have been a difficult task since it was listed in the student directory. She also said that she was not a member of any political action organizations, clubs, or movements on or off campus.

"I'm telling you, Dad, you are totally misjudging Walid. He is a fine young man with a good heart and I know he had nothing to do with this whole nightmare."

"Maybe not," Alon replied, "but he is the one who ran from the scene and hasn't been found since. You'd think that with such a good heart, he might be here to help us."

Alon turned to Nadev and repeated the initial question. As expected, the response was more argumentative than cooperative.

"Look Dad," he said, "I'm not a criminal so I resent this kind of interrogation, especially from a parent without any real legal jurisdiction here."

"Nadev," Alon snapped, "for once in your life, try hard to be with me and not an adversary to everything I say. I'm telling you, this thing is serious and it's very possible the assassin was not in the apartment to see me, but for you. If you know something that might help us, tell me and spare me your bullshit attitudes because right now, I really don't care about them."

The little family conference ended with about as much success as it had when it started. Nadev returned to his room and his laptop computer. Sonya retreated to the couch with her cell phone. As for Alon, he grabbed a donut and left for another meeting with the two federal agents.

CHAPTER 22

"Nadev, are you almost ready?" Alon called.
"In a minute."
Nadev had a post-operative check-up visit at two o'clock that day with his surgeon. Alon was going to drive him there in Sonya's car. He told Sonya to stay at Rebecca's, where they would all meet for dinner.

The ride to see Dr. Green took about thirty minutes. Alon asked Nadev how his surgical site felt, but otherwise they drove in silence. In the doctor's waiting room, Alon picked up a magazine to pass the time. When Nadev's name was finally called, the two men followed a nurse's assistant to the designated room. She directed Nadev to remove his shirt in order to fully expose his injured arm. Though Nadev would have preferred his father remain in the waiting room, Alon was adamant about staying and hearing what the doctor had to say.

After a few minutes, Dr. Green entered the room accompanied by a young medical resident. He introduced the resident, greeted Alon and focused his attention on his patient. "So, Nadev, how are you doing?"

"Fine," Nadev muttered, in a short tone of voice.

Dr. Green, ignored the hostile response. He had worked with plenty of patients like Nadev who had every reason to be angry about the injuries that brought them to this office. As the doctor examined the amputation site he voiced his observations for the benefit of the student doctor as well as the patient and his father. "No signs of infection or other complication. The site is healing well with mild redness and inflammation." As he further examined the site, Nadev flinched, reflexively withdrawing his stump from the doctor's grasp. Dr. Green continued with his verbal dictation. "There is moderate discomfort and a slight opening with minimal drainage on the distal medial border of the incision on the right arm." He instructed the resident doctor to swab the drainage, obtain a culture and to re-dress the wound site. "Nadev," Dr. Green said, "I'm going to write you a prescription for an oral antibiotic. You're to take it three times a day, as directed, for the next ten days. It will prevent or cure any lingering infection. Use it all, even if you're feeling better."

"Mr. Levy," he said to Alon, "please wait outside the room for a few moments. I'll be with you shortly."

Alon left the room to give the doctor time to have a private discussion with Nadev. Ten minutes later Dr. Green came out alone. "Your son's physical status is quite good," he said. "Things are progressing well. I don't suspect any infection, but I'm playing it safe with the antibiotic. On a related note, I must ask, are things alright at home? Forgive me for prying. I'm not a psychiatrist, but it's obvious Nadev is full of anger, and a lot of it seems directed towards you. He has some deep-seated feelings that seem to have nothing to do with the explosion or his missing arm."

Alon took a deep breath. "My son and I have a very poor relationship, as you have probably surmised. I accept most of the responsibility and attribute it to my inadequacy as a parent. My job has drawn me away from my home and family on an unpredictable basis. When my children were growing up, I was frequently absent. My wife was at home taking care of issues I should have managed. When she died of leukemia three years ago, the situation got worse. I addressed my grief by becoming more involved in my work than ever before. That was when I began to notice Nadev's growing anger and resentment toward me. He would try his damnedest to irritate me, and he knows the right buttons to push!"

"I hold myself responsible for not being a good parent. I know I shortchanged my children. But my work is not the normal nine-to-five job. I work when national or local crises arise in my country; crises that require my complete attention, and I work until the problem or issue is resolved. My daughter seems to understand this, but my son never has. He resents what I do, why I do it, and what could happen if I don't do it. It is difficult, Dr. Green, to commit oneself to protecting the security of your country when your own son doesn't care whether you come home alive or not."

"I see. Have you tried reaching out to him and explaining yourself?"

"Many times. But once we start talking, things heat up very quickly."

"Have you considered professional counseling?"

"On two occasions, I tried the professional help route for both of us. The result was I ended up alone in the therapy room and my son sat in the car waiting for me."

"For what it's worth, Mr. Levy," the doctor said, "I suggest you not be so hard on yourself. You may not have been the perfect parent, but then, who is? From what you've told me, I'm sure you're faced with challenges few of us ever encounter. With the loss of your wife, you did what a lot of people do. You treated your grief by immersing yourself into your work. One day Nadev, with time, understanding, and maturity will be more willing to establish a better relationship with you. I'd bet on it!"

"Thanks, I appreciate your concern."

"Well, getting back to your son's physical condition, bring him back for a recheck in about two weeks. If things continue to improve, we'll clear him for a prosthetic fitting and discuss his return to Israel.

Chapter 23

Alon drove to the Federal building for the scheduled review session with the two FBI field agents. The three of them sat at the conference table sipping coffee and nibbling at day-old cookies on a paper plate. They made small talk, and then turned their attention to the contents of a file labeled "evidence review." Agent Cramden began by reading the evidence on the intruder at Sonya's apartment. As expected, the fingerprints obtained from the deceased had no matchup for anyone with a criminal record. The weapon used was a Beretta, reported stolen two years earlier. The intruder appeared Middle Eastern, in his early thirties, with no identification of any sort. The soft, clean skin on his hands indicated that he didn't work at manual labor. Agent Cramden related that one of his men was watching the funeral home in case anyone came to pick up the man's personal articles...his watch, two rings, a chain necklace and clothing.

Next was a discussion about the explosion site. Two more critically injured patrons died bringing the death count to thirteen...a good day's work for a terrorist. Walid Kassab was still missing with no new leads in sight. "We still believe he is in the area hiding, or is being hidden locally. We have people everywhere and feel confident that we will find him soon," Kurnitz said.

Cramden chimed in with additional forensic evidence recently added to the file. "From the explosive's concentric pattern evident at the site, it would appear the bomb went off in this area." He pointed to the diagram showing table arrangements and the labeled names of patrons in their approximate positions. "Our forensic studies also showed small fragments of nylon shreds, fibers, and other threaded materials spread out in a 360 degree direction from the central site of the blast."

"Do you know what those fiber fragments are and where they came from?" inquired Alon.

"Not sure," Cramden replied. "They're badly charred, and undoubtedly they're from whatever covered the explosive substance."

Alon sat and stared for several minutes at the evidence file and then the diagrammatic chart.

Rebecca grew increasingly uncomfortable with the silence and said, "Come on, Alon. Tell us what's on your mind."

"Nothing really," he replied. "Just a thought. I'll mull it over to see if it makes sense. If so, I'll pass it on to you."

The conversation turned to Nadev's medical condition and the information provided by Dr. Green. Once Nadev received his prosthetic arm and had a round of physical therapy to comfortably use it, he would be able to return to Israel.

That night, shortly after dinner, Sonya asked to speak with her father alone. The two went into an empty bedroom and sat down. "I have something important to tell you, but before I do, you need to promise me that whatever I reveal is between us, and you will not contact the authorities about it. Will you promise me that?"

"Yes, I promise. You can feel safe about whatever it is."

"Okay, Dad. I heard from Walid this afternoon. He called me on my cell from a public pay phone."

Alon's eyes lit up, but he held his excitement in check.

"What did he say?"

"He told me he didn't cause the explosion, and he no longer wants to be the target of a major man hunt by the authorities for something he didn't do."

"Do you have some way of reaching him?"

"Yes, at two o'clock today, he's going to call me for further information."

"What sort of information?"

"He wants to meet and talk with you before considering what to do. He also wants me there as a sort of protection...from you."

"Sonya, listen to me. Walid is a prime suspect in a terrorist bombing that resulted in many deaths, terrible injuries, and the destruction of a building, not to mention the devastation of the involved families and friends. He needs to turn himself in and quickly. If he didn't do it, he should have no fear of explaining himself to the authorities."

"Dad, it's not that simple."

"It can't get any simpler."

"Walid insists his best chance for justice and safety is to talk with you and me...alone, before going to the authorities. He's afraid of you, but he trusts you to hear his explanation. He wants me there as a buffer. The only thing he insists on is that you give your word you will not contact the authorities until after hearing him out."

Alon thought about it for a moment. "Alright Sonya, I'm cautious, but I will meet with him with one exception...you will not be there. I will not agree in any way to jeopardize your safety for the sake of making him more comfortable. If he won't meet with me alone and explain himself, the deal is off the table and he'll be out there on his own."

"Dad, you have to see his point!"

"No, I don't. I've heard your request on Walid's behalf and I've told you what I'm willing to do. Talk to him and explain it well, because that's the only way it will be done!"

Sonya knew when her father was through negotiating and that point had been reached. As she turned to leave the bedroom, Alon said, "One more thing. Do not mention either this conversation or your talk with Walid to Rebecca. She is a good person, and now a dear friend, but she is also a Federal agent. So for the time being, the less she knows about this particular issue, the better."

Less than thirty minutes after Alon's conversation with Sonya, his cell phone rang. It was Rebecca calling from the office with some very interesting news. A young man in his late twenties by the name of Saeed Mohomaddi had picked up the personal items of the deceased intruder at the hospital morgue. He signed his name, showed a license for verification, and left with a plastic bag containing a watch, two rings, a pair of shoes and a chain link necklace. Additional good news was that an FBI field agent was watching the area and followed Mohomaddi to a second floor apartment. Twenty-four hour surveillance by an FBI mobile unit was immediately established. Rebecca relayed the street address where the man had gone and Alon memorized the information for later recall.

Alon asked Rebecca if the pick-up guy had been identified on any of the watch lists or international investigation groups. Her answer was that the data was still being processed and further information would be forthcoming. She then proposed to meet Alon for lunch. He declined, saying he had to take care of personal matters. In fact, his personal matter was to be around the apartment when Sonya heard next from Walid.

Alon's next phone call was to Yosef. He repeated to him the correct address of the pick-up man. Alon picked a Starbucks coffee shop on 8th Street and Barlin Avenue where he and Yosef could meet at 4 p.m. the following day. He told Yosef to run a check on the pick-up man and to think of a way to distract or eliminate the FBI surveillance of the apartment, if necessary, at a later time. Alon instructed Yosef to tell him right away of any other comings and goings of either residents or visitors to Mohomaddi's apartment building. Other plans could wait until he and Yosef met.

Alon waited anxiously at Rebecca's house while Nadev and Sonya sat together in the den talking in subdued tones. He knew it was essential for him to meet Walid. If they had a productive talk he might be willing to surrender peacefully and give essential information as to who had planned the bombing, supplied the explosive, and their motives. At 2:05 p.m., the house was quiet. Another five minutes passed with no call. Then, with the bright sounds of classical music on her cellular phone, the call came. Sonya answered it and signaled her father that it was Walid. She put him on speaker and explained that her father was willing to meet, but he was adamant that she not be there. She pleaded with her friend to keep the meeting. After some discussion, he agreed. They would meet at 7 p.m. that evening behind the large dumpster on the south side of Jefferson Middle School. No other people were to be within eyesight of the meeting place and Alon was to be unarmed or the meeting would not take place. Alon listened to the details and nodded his acceptance.

Chapter 24

The Meeting

Before his meeting with Walid, Alon gave a lot of thought to notifying Rebecca and letting the FBI take over the arranged interaction. Ultimately, curiosity got the better of him. He wanted to hear what the young man had to say. The FBI would close in like an army on the attack. Armed agents, local cops, swat teams and trained snipers would all be part of the mix, and inherent mishaps could mean another man would not make it to questioning. It was better for him to listen to Walid's explanation alone before bringing in the big guns. Early on, Alon felt sure that Walid was the perpetrator. Now he felt a trace of doubt. If the youth was, in fact, the bomber, why did he request the meeting? It was a good question and so far, there was no apparent answer.

Alon was not foolish. He had no intention of going unarmed as he had initially promised. He concealed a .45 caliber Beretta handgun in a leather holster in the back waistline of his pants and also carried a small .38 caliber pistol in a right ankle holster. Yes, he had given his word to both Walid and Sonya that he would not carry a gun, but this kind of meeting required special precautions. Alon had no idea of what to expect. All he knew was that Kassab was on the run, desperate, and involved in this mess to some extent. They would meet. He would hear Kassab's story, and take him into custody when it was over.

Walid glanced at his watch. It read 6:54 p.m. He eyed the designated dumpster from his lookout position on the roof of the school and became aware of someone approaching the side of the building. He had no doubt the man in the black winter parka was Alon Levy, Sonya's father. Attached to the side of the school was a flat, metal ladder that could be slid up or down to the ground, preventing students from climbing to the roof from the ground level. He put his foot on the first rung, started his decent to the ground, and called out, "Mr. Levy, is that you?"

"Yes," Alon answered.

"I'm Walid Kassab, Mr. Levy, public enemy number one." He stepped off the ladder and walked over to Alon, reached into his coat pocket, withdrew a small handgun and aimed it at him.

Alon raised his hands. "Whoa there! Don't do anything you might regret. You told me no weapons. I honored your demand, and now you're pointing that pistol at me. What's going on?"

Walid's hand shook. He blurted out with panic in his voice, "I didn't do it, Mr. Levy. I had nothing to do with that whole thing. I swear it!"

"Really? Your explanation would carry more validity if you put away that gun."

"Okay," Walid said weakly, pocketing the weapon. "I'm sorry. I would never have hurt you anyway. I was just using it to scare you into being less aggressive. Sonya told me all about you, and, I, I just thought the gun would even things out."

Alon smiled. "Walid, you're either an honest kid caught up in a giant mess or one hell of an idiot who could easily get himself killed."

"What do you mean?"

"Let's start with you threatening me with an old .22 caliber pistol that shoots blanks and is used as a starting gun for track meets and swim races. If that's not stupidity, then consider meeting someone behind a school dumpster and watching his arrival from the roof of the school. You left yourself no safe exit route and in truth, made your capture easy. Now let's turn to the meat and potatoes of this meeting. I came to hear your side of the story. There have been a lot of confusing questions about your involvement in the delicatessen bombing and frankly, it doesn't look good. So, answer my questions with the truth and let's see where we're at."

The two of them cleared snow off of a nearby picnic table and sat on the benches across from one another. Walid, looking glum, asked Alon, "How did you know about the fake gun?"

"Because, you dumb shit, weapons are a part of my life and when you look closely, you'll see the barrel is not even fully opened. You were holding a cap gun. Now, let's get on with what happened that day."

Walid told his story beginning with sitting at one of the deli tables with Denise. Nadev then joined them once he entered the restaurant. "After Nadev excused himself to go to the bathroom, I went over to the cashier's stand and asked to speak to a manager. I was standing there waiting when the blast threw me against one of the counters."

"Why did you want to speak to the manager?"

"I was so sick and tired of commercial establishments raising funds to donate to Israel while ignoring the Palestinians and other troubled Arab nations."

Alon pondered if Walid was telling the truth or spouting bullshit. "After the blast, were you unconscious, or aware of what was going on around you?"

"I was dazed, dizzy, and deaf as a stone, but I was never unconscious."

"What happened next?"

"Well, when I got up, I looked around and it was horrible! Body parts everywhere, blood, screaming, people moaning in pain! There was heavy debris and smoke filling my lungs, choking me. I couldn't breathe. My mouth was filled with plaster particles. And what I saw around me made me want to vomit. I kept stumbling toward the light to get outside of the restaurant. On the way, I stopped at the table where I had been sitting and saw...it was...my friend, Denise." He stopped to take a deep breath and compose himself. "She, what was left of her, was spread out...she was...in pieces. I had just been sitting there!"

Alon said, "Go on. What happened next?"

"When I got to the outside, there were people helping the survivors. At the EMS treatment vehicle site, they put the seriously injured on gurneys to take them to the hospital. While I was being patched up, the attendant mentioned to me that the authorities, and I think he mentioned specifically the FBI, would need to collect information from me about the bombing. As soon as he left the vehicle, I took off into the crowd."

"Hmmm, they fixed you up and then you ran away. Why? You must have known that after this kind of event it's standard procedure to interview all of the survivors, find out what they know. By running, you made yourself a prime suspect."

"There was a reason I left the scene and I'd rather keep it to myself. I promise you, I had nothing to do with the explosion."

Alon studied the boy, and in a low, serious voice said, "Walid, we are at a pivotal split in the road. You either win me over as a believer or turn me into your worst enemy. You're past the point of keeping essential information to yourself. Get it all out. Tell me why you ran."

Walid told how at the age of fourteen he was selected and sent to a training camp operated by a radical Islamic Jihadist group. He had volunteered to go for six months of indoctrination in return for his family receiving financial aid and other rewards. Better food, housing, and job assignments for his family were all part of the package. "Once I got to the camp, it didn't take long to realize the purpose of the training and education. You ate, slept and lived every moment of the day with the ideology of hating Jews and the state of Israel. Even the geographic maps of the Middle East had a blackened rectangle covering Israel to reinforce the fact that it didn't exist. Jews had taken the land and were living on Arabic sand and soil illegally without the blessing of our God, Allah. I was able to see the camp for what it was and left after my six-month obligation. During that time, I never did anything illegal or harmful to anyone. I was afraid if the FBI interviewed me, I felt sure they would be able to bring up my past political affiliation. As an Egyptian college student, I'd lose my scholarship and probably face deportation. Also, my time at the camp would blemish my past. I couldn't take a chance of crushing my career aspirations, so I ran to avoid the inevitable trouble."

Alon was not a man easily swayed by prepared excuses or stories. In addition, he had no particular love for young Egyptian men who joined anti-Jewish hate groups hell bent on the destruction and elimination of Israel. However, exceptions did exist and Alon, listening to his gut, believed Walid and his explanation. The kid ran from the scene at the wrong time for a valid reason.

Walid held his head in his hands and cried like a baby. His pent-up emotions needed release. Alon moved to the other side of the bench and put an arm around the young man's shoulders. Walid pressed into Alon like a child clinging to his father.

"I'm sorry, Mr. Levy, I'm so sorry," he whimpered.

"I know. I think in the long run, everything will work out and you'll be alright. Where have you been hiding where no one could find you?"

"I've been staying in the boiler room in the school's basement. I never left during the day and bought food at a nearby 7-11 at night. I got into the place through a window and slept on the cement ground with a blanket." He brushed his hand over his eyes to wipe away his tears.

"I believe you," Alon said. "I'm going to take you to Sonya's apartment until I can work out some details. Sonya and Nadev are with me at another location temporarily. Now, you've got to give me your word that you will stay at her apartment and call no one including my kids until I come to get you. Is that understood?"

Walid gave his word and thanked Alon for believing his explanation and for helping him.

Alon patted the boy on the back and said, "You see, we Jews from Israel are not all devils."

Walid replied, "And we Egyptians aren't all terrorists either!"

Chapter 25

As Alon walked through the front door of Rebecca's house, he was met by Sonya and Nadev in the foyer. Sonya eagerly inquired about his meeting with Walid.

Nadev asked, "Is he still breathing?"

Alon gave his son a disgusted look that spoke volumes, turned to his daughter and said, "Walid is fine. For now, and for the sake of his safety and security, I've put him at your apartment. I've instructed him to not go out or phone anyone. And don't either of you try to contact him. Once his location is compromised, I will not be able to help him. Do you both understand the situation?" The two nodded their heads in agreement.

"What was his explanation?" asked Sonya. "I mean, I was right, wasn't I? Walid had nothing to do with it."

"His explanation seemed reasonable, but it's not quite ready for the authorities to hear. You'll have to take my word on this and understand I am trying to help him. I'll tell you the whole story soon. Trust me. We all have to keep him and his story secret."

"So he actually is alive," Nadev commented.

"That's not funny," Alon said.

"It wasn't meant as a joke. You do have a certain reputation, you know. It seems like whenever you work on an assignment, people get hurt. Back home, the response is admiration and recognition by our government."

"You have very little knowledge of what I do on the job," Alon fired back, "and have never shown much interest in learning about it. Perhaps if you did, your misguided and insensitive attitudes would change."

"I doubt that. I know only too well about your job responsibilities and your stellar performance, and I'm not impressed."

Alon's anger flared. He tried to tolerate his son's remarks by blaming them on his medications. His toleration had limits and Nadev was on the edge. "What's wrong with you, Nadev? Your remarks make you sound like being a *putz* is a virtue."

"As always, Father, my opinions mean nothing and your spoken words are law. Israel is a country full of Alon Levys. You all think alike, act alike, and push your ideological nonsense on anyone who will listen. I am 21 years old and a man, and I am tired of being a silent follower of the Alon Levy way of life."

"Nadev," Alon said, "you are 21 years old, but far from being a man. If you feel such hatred of our present lifestyle in Israel, you should do something about it."

"What are my options, Mr. Mossad?"

"For starters you could leave the country and make your home elsewhere. When we return to Israel, you can pack your bags and do just that. Your choice."

"Maybe I will." Nadev rose from his chair and stormed out of the room.

Alon needed to visit Walid. He planned to buy some food and assorted articles for him. But most of all, Alon needed distance from his son. As a father, he hated himself for having said what he did. It was hard for him to get along with his child. It was as if the two of them were not meant to be together.

Walid was sitting on the couch watching television when Alon came in carrying two bags of groceries. He got up to help Alon and asked how long he would have to stay isolated in the apartment. Alon told him there were details to work out that would take another day or two. The important thing, he told Walid, was that before taking him in to the authorities, he wanted to have another suspect. Or better still, a confirmed confession so that Walid would be seen as innocent of any crime.

That evening, Alon had dinner with Walid in Sonya's apartment. His confrontation with Nadev still bothered him and he needed to talk about his estranged relationship with his son.

"What angers you most about Nadev?" Walid asked.

"It's that ideological bullshit attitude of his and his lack of respect or gratitude for the life he has in Israel. Everything we do, everything we attempt to improve is never right or good enough for him. Do you know what I mean?"

"Yes, I do. I'm Egyptian and I'm sure many of my thoughts are contrary to those held by you and other Israelis. I would hope you feel no disapproval of me or my family."

"I understand. You were born an Egyptian. I may not agree with all of your thoughts and beliefs, but I can certainly respect how you got them. They are products of your upbringing and family heritage. I would expect as a son that you would respect your parents and not despise their very existence. It is the same in our case. Nadev was born and raised as an Israeli Jew. I don't expect him to agree with all of our policies, traditions, and rules of daily life. But I do expect him to respect his parents, his friends, and his way of life. When you lose that respect, it's probably time to move on. I think Nadev is at that point in his life"

Walid nodded. "Lately, I also find myself having mixed feelings about my father. I lay awake at night thinking about a parent's relationship and obligations to their children. My father recently did something I'm having great difficulty accepting. My mother sent me an email message that upset me a lot. My brother Saran, was arrested by the Egyptian police and taken into custody. My loving father was the one that turned him in to the authorities. How could he do such a thing?"

"What was Saran charged with?"

"He was involved with a radical group making bombs and attaching detonators. I know, it sounds terrible, and I am entirely against it. Saran would never set off such a destructive weapon. He is not a violent person, and is still and always will be my brother. I'm sure you don't want to hear this, Mr. Levy, but if Saran did not assemble bomb devices, ten others would gladly take his place. My father claims Allah would not condone such work and that incarceration would at least keep my brother alive. How do I deal with this? I love my brother, and cannot believe my father did this thing."

Alon laid a comforting hand on Walid's shoulder. "Allah is your name for God. The taking of innocent lives to impose one country's political views upon another is not a product of good religious teachings. If one makes a bomb knowing its purpose and potential effects, he is just as responsible as the person who delivers it and sacrifices his life when it detonates. If anything, you should admire your father for having the God-given convictions and personal strength to do what he did. He is a brave man and deserves your respect and admiration. As a father, his decision must have been agonizing, and will probably torment him for the rest of his life. Think about it—he was trying to save lives, prevent massive destruction, and pay homage to the moral and virtuous teachings of his religion, the dictates of the Quran. You should be proud to be his son."

"Thank you for your explanation. I'll try to look at things, as you say, through different eyes."

Alon took his time driving back to Rebecca's house. It was 9:30 p.m. when he pulled into her driveway. Rebecca met him at the door, hugged him, and whispered in his ear, "I heard you had an uncomfortable afternoon here with Nadev."

"Sonya told you."

"Yes."

"And how did she feel about it?"

"Sonya feels Nadev has changed a lot since they were together in Israel. She feels his political views have somehow taken over his personal life. To talk with him is to argue with him or to accept his viewpoint as the truth."

"Other than that, how was your day?"

"At a standstill. No sign of Walid Kassab, and the Section Director is becoming more frustrated each day by our lack of progress."

That evening, Alon and Rebecca sat at the dining room table, drinking wine and talking. Alon opened up about his role as a father, and how he coped after his wife died. "My military involvement became my emotional and psychological outlet. I was neither physically or emotionally there for my children when they needed me. Yet, Sonya, by the grace of God, became a happy, social, well-adjusted young adult. Nadev didn't weather the storm as well as she. He is filled with resentment and anger, and with altered views on society, the government, and specifically, Israeli politics."

Rebecca sat and listened quietly. When he finished, she looked at him and said, "Alon, there's no reason to beat yourself up over your son. You're a good father. Yes, your particular line of work demands an unusual commitment. And I'm sure that before long Nadev will mature and learn to appreciate you, what you do, and his way of life."

CHAPTER 26

House Call

For the next two days, Alon Levy spent most of his time at Rebecca's taking care of Nadev and performing much needed home repair jobs. Alon had always been handy with basic repairs such as electrical, plumbing, and painting skills but unfortunately, not passed along to his children. Nadev needed less rest and was more able to move around the house. Three times each week, a physical therapist came and worked with him on strengthening exercises, pain control techniques, and limb loss re-education procedures. As soon as Rebecca and Sonya left the house, a mood of increased tension, hostility, and negativism arose in their absence. Alon tried hard to accept Nadev's attitudes, but their relationship continued to worsen. The answer for Alon, at least temporarily, was to leave the house and stay away for several hours while Nadev read, watched television, or became absorbed working on his laptop computer.

In the latter part of the afternoon, Alon would go over to Sonya's apartment and spend a couple of hours with Walid. He would take food and personal items to make his stay at the apartment more tolerable. The two Middle Easterners would sit at the kitchen table and discuss everything from politics to family matters and from career aspirations to friendship issues. A strange kind of bond began to form between them. Still, Alon's mind was restless. He knew the bomber would have to surface soon in order to ensure Walid's safety and declaration of innocence.

One early afternoon, Rebecca called and offered to take Alon out to dinner that night. She also wanted to update him on new information from the investigation. Alon accepted, and they agreed to meet at La Mer, a trendy French restaurant. Sonya wasted no time in advising her father what to wear, how to act, which subjects to talk about and which ones to avoid. "Calm down, Sonya," Alon said. "This is a dinner and not a proposal of marriage."

Dinner at La Mer meant great seafood, a quiet ambience, and good service. They were not disappointed. After a shared dessert, Rebecca produced a thin manila folder. She opened it and said, "We found a computer site active in recruiting young people into various radical Islamic support groups. We're getting a warrant to arrest the source operator and confiscate the involved computers, but an actual conviction is going to be difficult—freedom of speech and all that. The source is from a Chicago residence, and we've located an address."

"Do you think there's a link between this recruiting site and the restaurant explosion?"

"It's a possibility, and shutting down the site is a priority. If nothing else, it will show them we are aware of their operation and are monitoring it closely."

Alon narrowed his eyes in thought. "Listen, I have an idea. Hear me out before you reject the concept. Some situations are better off being handled not strictly by the book. Right now you think it is in your best interest to shut down this computer site as soon as possible. But what would that accomplish? You arrest whoever is operating the site only to set him free in a matter of hours. You'll confiscate the hard drive information, but eventually run into a lot of dead ends and bad links to non-existent organizations. The bottom line is the site, or another one just like it, will be up and operational again in a few days. You lose, our computer recruiter is inconvenienced but wins, and the search for better and more viable evidence goes on. There is another approach."

"I'm listening," Rebecca said. "Remember though, this is America, not Israel. We cannot break laws for the purpose of building a better case."

Alon pressed his case. "Let's look at this computer situation as an opportunity, not just a way to inconvenience a potential terrorist recruiter. I say that you allow me and a certain associate with specialized computer talents to make a short visit to the site. First, we copy the information off the hard drive for investigative purposes. Then we install a cyber virus with a timed release into the operative's computer that will encrypt the computer data making it unreadable, and spread along the existing communication links to alter their information banks as well. By the time they, whoever they are, detect and destroy the computer virus, massive damage to their information and memory banks will have been accomplished. Now, how is that for causing them some serious shit?"

There was a brief period of silence as Rebecca pondered the proposal. "Although the concept is sound, there's no way I could even consider taking part in that kind of scheme. It reeks of illegality and would certainly spell the end of my career in law enforcement. I shouldn't even be here listening to this kind of talk. You should know better."

"Of course," Alon said. "I'm aware of the legal issues breached by this kind of operation. I would never ask you to condone, take part in, or otherwise have anything to do with this plan. As far as you and I are concerned, this conversation never took place. What I am doing is informing you of what needs to be done. I have an associate in this area who's a wizard with computers. He is also an active Mossad agent, and will follow my exact directions. No one will be hurt. We can copy hard drive data and install a cyber virus within 15 to 20 minutes. All I need is for you to place the address of the operative site on the table and leave the room for a few seconds. You have no knowledge of what we plan to do and have no part in carrying out the operation."

"How do I know no one will get hurt?"

"You tell me when your people intend on picking up this operative and confiscating the hard drive information and I'll have the job completed prior to them ever entering the door. Personally, I would prefer you leave him alone, and let the operation continue as usual. Our people will watch the residence and only enter once the operative leaves the site. No contact, altercation, or violence will occur. You have my word on that."

"Alon, if I do this, I may want to review the information on the hard drive, but want nothing containing electronic data. Is that understood? I don't want the possibility of an electronic trail back to me. I would insist on that."

"Absolutely. You have to understand, Becky, the greatest impact we could have on this recruiting process would be for them not to realize we know about it. The implanted computer virus will activate and spread within hours. The less they know or even suspect, the better the effect."

"I'll see what I can do. However, at best I think I will only be able to postpone our involvement. Cancelling the arrest would raise suspicions. The arrest, search and seizure are planned for tomorrow morning at ten o'clock. You cannot count on my delaying the operation. Here is the address of the site." Rebecca tossed a folder marked "Operation in Process," on the tabletop.

"I hope to God, Alon," she said, "I won't regret this. My heart tells me it needs to be done, but as a law enforcement officer, I worry...bigtime."

Alon put his arm around Rebecca's shoulder. "Those recruiting computer sites prey on young adults who are often confused, depressed, socially awkward, or in search of some new beginning. Once the selection process and necessary indoctrination are completed, one or more of these young recruits may become your next suicide bomber. If you can play a part in preventing that from happening, I'd call it a good day for Agent Kurnitz!"

Rebecca excused herself to gaze at the colorful artwork placed around the restaurant, giving Alon a chance to pick up the folder and memorize the street address of the computer site. He set the folder back on the table, grabbed his jacket and paid the bill, winking at Becky as he left. Once outside, he dialed Yosef's phone number.

It didn't take long for Alon to explain the plan to Yosef and to enlist his assistance. Yosef gathered what he needed to complete the task and sent a subordinate to provide surveillance of the designated address, and to notify Alon when the house was vacated. Alon picked up Yosef and the two waited for the desired phone call.

Yosef said, "This is an interesting idea, but it makes me wonder what has happened to you over time."

"What do you mean?"

"I mean, we have done a lot of things as a team over the years. The Alon Levy I have always known would just as easily have entered this house in question, destroyed the computer, burned the records and put a bullet in the bastard's head. But now, we're sneaking around, waiting for someone to leave so we can insert a cyber virus into a computer hard drive."

"Yosef," Alon chuckled, "sometimes you think with your ass. In case you hadn't noticed, this is not Israel. Different rules. For this particular case, it's our best choice. American justice will have this bastard back on the streets and operational within days. Your computer virus will encrypt their data and spread it along the electronic channels resulting in the corruption and subsequent deletion of other data sources. Is it winning the war? Of course not. They'll find it, destroy it, and reopen for business. Our act will hurt them, slow them down temporarily, and let them know they cannot operate freely without the fear of consequences."

As Alon finished his explanation, the phone rang. A middle-aged male had just left the house, gotten into his car, and drove off in a northerly direction. Alon instructed Yosef's associate to follow the car at a safe distance and to notify the agents if and when he headed back.

The next part went smoothly. Yosef picked the side door lock and used a special type of meter to detect the presence of an alarm system with or without motion detectors. Fortunately, there was no alarm system on the premise. They quickly searched the house and found a basement office with two desktop computers. Yosef went to work. Alon roamed the house looking for any other articles of interest and found none. Both men wore surgical gloves to eliminate the possibility of fingerprint identification. Yosef was an artist at his work. He downloaded the existing files onto a quality, high capacity flash drive, and then planted a cyber virus onto each of the two hard drives. Once activated, the time-released virus would wreak havoc on any involved computer system.

Yosef finished his work in less than fifteen minutes. The two exited the side door and relocked it. They got into their car and drove away. The time release was set for one hour and Alon felt a special sense of accomplishment. Yosef called his associate and learned the male under surveillance had gone to meet two other friends at a restaurant and had not left. He told him to return to Yosef's house. Once there, the three men sat in the study while Yosef printed off the data downloaded from the recruitment site. The information was revealing. It contained names, addresses, and contact information of responding individuals primarily from the mid-western region of the United States. The data also contained email communications between the recruiter and inquiring individuals. As expected, many of the messages indicated existing problems, emotional instability, and social frustrations at the homes of the potential candidates. As a parent, Alon wondered if the parents of those applicants had any idea what their children were considering. The answer was obvious though and Alon felt a guarded sense of mixed empathy for the recruited individuals as well as their families.

Alon sent a text message to Rebecca thanking her for the previous night's dinner. The dinner acknowledgement was a pre-arranged coded message that signified the mission had been completed. Alon smiled to himself. There was considerable satisfaction in a good day's work.

CHAPTER 27

Alon arrived the next morning at the Federal Building for his regularly scheduled meeting with Agents Cramden and Kurnitz. He sat in silence while listening to Cramden report on the surveillance involving the acquaintance of the assassin, which failed to produce any viable information. Federal officers were sent to investigate Saeed Mohomaddi to try and establish a connection to the intruder. They discovered the two middle Easterners were friends. Mohomaddi had merely picked up the man's personal articles after reading about the incident in the newspaper. In his comments to the authorities, Mohomaddi expressed surprise and said he had no knowledge of why his friend had done what he did, which of course, was completely out of character.

The FBI obtained no useful information on Mohomaddi other than he had a roommate, and the surveillance operation was cancelled. The two agents were still convinced that their number one suspect was the Egyptian student, Walid Kassab. Alon wanted desperately to tell them that Walid was innocent, but held back until the real terrorist was apprehended.

Early that evening, Alon met Yosef and Jacob Roth, one of his associates, at a local community library. They went into one of the private study cubicles and closed the door. Alon briefly summarized the available evidence as well as personal impressions. He told Yosef and Jacob about his encounter and discussion with Kassab. Alon made it clear that he believed Kassab had nothing to do with the explosion. "When we locate the explosives supplier," Alon said, we'll have the culprit."

Alon reviewed with Yosef and his associate the factual evidence pertaining to the intruder and the confrontation at Sonya's apartment.

Alon felt sure the break-in and assassination attempt were related to the terrorist incident at Sid's Delicatessen. "Then, an Iranian immigrant, Saeed Mohomaddi, in the United States for less than two years, picked up the personal remains of the dead assassin from the hospital morgue and claimed to be only a friend of the intruder, who was also an Irani. Mohomaddi lives in a small apartment with another supposedly unrelated Iranian friend. Both were checked for terrorism ties and came up clean. I have a hunch the two were a local terrorist group cell, possibly tied into the supply and training of whoever delivered the bomb."

Alon laid out his next plan to Yosef and his associate. First, he needed Yosef to prepare identification badges and wallet-sized cards showing that the three of them were agents from the Homeland Security Division. That would get them into Mohomaddi's apartment. A fake search warrant would allow search and seizure of their cell phones, computer hard drives, and apartment. Alon, at that point, would present bogus evidence of the explosive military grade C4 substance in the hopes of obtaining a confession, with no consequences in return for information on the bomber. The plan was risky—fake IDs, phony evidence, unauthorized promises, and an illegal search, but if the subjects took the bait, the entire operation would prove itself worthwhile, according to Mossad standards anyway.

Yosef kept nodding his head in agreement and said he would create the papers, including the badges, by early evening. "Do we go in armed as usual, Alon?" he asked.

"Of course we do. Hopefully, we won't need to use force but one never knows what might come up."

"Count me in," Roth said. "I'll be ready."

Yosef asked Alon, "What exactly are we looking for with the cell phones and hard drives?"

"Repeated communications to any recognizable cell phone numbers or email messages to someone about a particular pick-up prior to the date of the explosion. Most important would be their response to our bluff on having found evidence of C4 in their apartment. If they deny it, then we're out the door with our tails between our legs. If they talk, we could hit the jackpot."

"Assuming the papers will be ready later today, when would you plan to carry out this operation?" Yosef asked.

"Tomorrow night, this library, at 7:30. Wear dark suits, black shoes, and nice conservative ties with white shirts," Alon stated. "After all, for tomorrow night anyway, we have to dress the role."

The three shook hands and left the library. On the way to the parking lot, Yosef asked Alon a question that had been on his mind. "How can you be so sure that this kid, Walid, had nothing to do with the bombing? Fifteen minutes alone in a room with him and we would have the truth."

"Yosef, my friend," replied Alon, "This is not years ago. Sometimes you know somebody well enough to realize his non-involvement."

"You've only known him a short time."

"It's not the quantity of time spent with him, but rather what and how he explained himself. Believe me, Yosef, if I'm good at anything, it's this. Kassab, had absolutely nothing to do with this tragedy other than having been there when it happened."

Yosef softened. "Who am I to question your impressions of a possible suspect? I'm sorry, Alon. I never meant to disrespect you. Please forgive me."

"Yosef, we are both men in the same profession. We work for Mossad. You are right to question me. Never think otherwise. And never apologize for it!"

They said good night and left for their respective vehicles. Alon headed home for what he hoped would be a peaceful meal with Rebecca and his two children. As he drove, his mind raced from one possible scenario to another involving the Iranians. Would they see through the bluff and stick to a story of innocence or take the bait and reveal their real purpose and identities? Also on his mind was his dysfunctional father/son relationship. There was no question that Alon had a plate full of crises and only a spoonful of possible solutions.

When Alon arrived home, he noticed Rebecca had set the dining room table for four. She had prepared a pot roast with assorted vegetables for dinner, trying to create a warm, familial ambiance. Sonya was in the kitchen helping Rebecca. Nadev was still in his room with the door closed. Alon told Sonya to get Nadev for dinner, and then he walked into the kitchen and thanked Rebecca for her efforts. He leaned in and kissed her on the cheek. Sonya returned and announced that Nadev was being difficult. He told her he wasn't hungry and had no interest in dining with his father. Rebecca asked, "Do you want to talk to Nadev and make peace?"

"No. I think I'll pass on that for now."

Dinner that night was tasty and attractively served. The three of them talked and laughed about things of little consequence, enjoying themselves while Nadev, once again, succeeded in distancing himself from his family with a sense of bitterness, disdain, and lack of respect.

CHAPTER 28

Unofficial Visit

It was a cold winter evening when the three Mossad agents met outside of the community library. They got into Yosef's Jeep Grand Cherokee and took a few moments to enjoy the heat. All three were wearing traditional U.S. government security outfits including a dark suit, white shirt, tie, and black shoes.

Alon reviewed the plan of operation with the others, stressing one point in particular—it was crucial to convince the occupants of the apartment that there would be no arrest or punitive action if they confessed and gave up the bomber's identity. That was the sole purpose of this mission. Failure would result from one of two scenarios: first, if they were innocent of wrong doing, and second, if they saw through their plot. Each of the men in the SUV carried a loaded handgun in an inside shoulder holster. All three weapons were Glocks and had the appearance of government-issue handguns. It was hoped there would be no reason to use them, but they carried them just in case.

At 7:00 p.m. sharp, the three self-appointed Homeland Security agents; Alon, Yosef, and Jacob, exited the car and approached the building where the two Iranians lived in apartment 202, two doors down from the elevator. Yosef held an official looking thin leather carrying case that contained several fabricated reports relating to this case. Alon, the team leader, would do most of the talking. Yosef's concern was that Alon would make sudden and drastic changes in his approach depending on how things were proceeding. He also realized that that kind of behavior was what made Alon so effective at these types of operations.

The solution was to keep quiet, follow his lead, and know that you were working with the best.

The doorbell rang and after a brief moment, a heavily accented male voice answered, "Who is there?"

Alon said, "Good evening, sir. I am Agent Lyle Brown and I have two fellow agents with me. We are from the Department of Homeland Security and we need to talk with you for a few minutes."

"About what?"

"That would be better discussed in the privacy of your home."

After a moment of silence, the man replied, "Okay, I'll buzz you in and you can come up."

Once the intercom connection was off, Alon turned and addressed his associates. "We're going to change our approach," he said with no explanation. "We enter military style, weapons out. Follow my lead."

The front door buzzed. They entered the foyer and ran up the stairs to the second floor. Each took out their weapon and released the safety. Alon knocked on door 202, announcing, "Agent Lyle Brown- Homeland Security."

The door knob turned and an Iranian man in his mid-thirties stood at the door. The three agents burst into the room, weapons drawn. A second man was seated in front of the television watching a soccer game. The man who opened the door was bewildered. "What is this?" he stammered. "What's going on here? Who are you?"

"Shut up and get down on the floor! On your knees!" Alon commanded as he shut the door with his foot.

"What is this all about? I demand that you answer me now," the man insisted as Jacob bound his hands.

"Shut the fuck up," Alon yelled. He pointed the gun at the man talking.

At the same time, Yosef went to the TV viewer and yanked him out of his chair. "Hands behind your back!" he commanded, and cuffed him with nylon restraints.

Alon pulled up a chair to be closer to the two captives and addressed them jointly. "What are your names?"

The talkative one answered, "I am Saeed Mohomaddi and my friend's name is Hassan Farahani. Now, I ask you, please, what have we done and why are you doing this to us?"

Alon spoke in a low tone, but without anger. He established their credibility by showing their security badges and placing an official looking search and seizure order on top of the coffee table. He then told the two men he had been ordered to confiscate their cell phones and computer hard drives. The phones were placed into a manila folder marked "Evidence" and sealed. Jacob went into a back room and began working on removing the hard drive from the desktop computer.

"Look fellas," Alon said, "We have a problem here. I'm sure we can find a solution without a lot of trouble if you cooperate. Our people did some testing in your apartment while you were out, and the results were positive for military C4. That means that recently, an amount of C4 explosive was in this apartment."

"No way! We never…"

Alon interrupted. "I told you to keep your mouth shut and listen. I won't say it again. Do you understand Saheed, Sahad, or whatever the fuck your name is?" Alon said, purposefully mispronouncing the man's name to emphasize that he was in control.

The man nodded.

"Now, back to the C4, which you seem to know about. Having that kind of shit in your possession, especially around the time of a terrorist bombing at a Jewish delicatessen here in Chicago is illegal and puts you two guys in the hot seat. But here's the good news. My superiors have given me permission to make you a one-time offer. Understand, we really don't give a shit about the two of you. We're willing to untie you and walk out the door on one condition. We want the bomber—the shithead that planted the bomb. Now, you're wondering if this offer is for real, and I probably would too if I were in your shoes." Alon reached into Yosef's carrying case and took out an official looking letter signed by a fictitious United States Attorney General as well as the director of Homeland Security.

"You'll notice this letter releases both of you from any arrest or criminal charges once the necessary information is obtained and verified. Your confession and the name of the actual terrorist who detonated the bomb are essential to your receiving this amnesty offer. Otherwise, I can proceed with arrest, interrogation and prosecution procedures." Alon sat back and waited.

Saeed asked to have his hands cut free so that he could properly read the documents. Instead, Jacob stood beside him and held the document for each of the two men, so they could read it.

"I want to understand this very clearly," Saeed said. "This is the government guaranteeing me and Hassan that if we give you the name of the alleged individual who allegedly picked up the alleged explosive and allegedly set it off, and admit that we supplied it to him, that we will in no way be held responsible for our alleged actions?"

Alon laughed dismissively. "Well, Saeed," he said. "there's a lot of alleging in that question. But yes, a free walk for your admission of involvement and for the name of the bomber. But only after he or she is proven to be the real deal."

Saeed leaned over to Hassan and they whispered in each other's ear in Farsi. Saeed frowned and he looked at his captors. "Alright,' he said, "we have a deal. We admit we supplied the package containing the explosive to a courier along with instructions on how to detonate the bomb. We were not the original source of the package, just middlemen between the original source and its final destination."

"Who was the original source of the explosive substance?"

"We have no idea, and that was not one of your requirements."

"Can we assume Iran might have been the source?"

"A fair assumption might be that my country, with infinite wisdom and religious guidance, may have played some role."

"And now, Saeed," Alon continued. "Give us the name of the courier who picked up the package and received your training."

Saeed sighed. "We don't have a name. We do not exchange names for obvious reasons. All we know is that he is a young male living here in Chicago."

"Keep talking."

"He was recruited over the Internet because of his Islamic Jihadist beliefs."

"Oh, shit!" Yosef, who was listening while reviewing the men's cell phone records, broke into a sweat. Everyone in the room stared his way.

"What's wrong?" Alon asked.

"You had better look at this."

Yosef handed him Saeed's cell phone. Nausea and shock shook Alon as he recognized the cell phone numbers as those of his son, Nadev.

He took a photo of Nadev from his wallet and thrust it in front of Saeed. "Look carefully," he said. "Is this the courier?"

"Yes. He's the one."

Alon's throat closed with tension. His whole world had suddenly turned upside down. He managed to mutter out loud that thirteen innocent men, women, and children had lost their lives in the explosion and many more were maimed or seriously injured.

Saeed responded, "Your government wreaks havoc and destruction on the people of the Middle East. You destroy our lands, attack our leaders, and reject the teachings of the prophet, Mohammed. We strike back with a small and unsophisticated response, and you call us terrorists and cowards. You tell me thirteen people were killed in the explosion and I say not enough, but certainly a good start!"

Alon snapped. He put the barrel of his gun to Saeed's forehead and squeezed the trigger without a moment's hesitation or remorse. The bullet hit Saheed's head like a rocket going through pudding. Blood, bone, and brains splattered on the back wall behind him. His eyes still open, Saeed lurched backwards from the impact and lay on the carpet, a pool of blood forming around his disfigured head.

Alon then turned to Hassan and once again raised the Glock and fired a bullet into the back of his head just below his left ear. He was dead before he hit the ground. Some of the gore landed on Yosef's suit.

"Alon!" Yosef cried.

"Take these two pieces of garbage and dump them in Lake Michigan as fish food," Alon growled. "I'll take the cell phones and for now, you guys hold on to the computer hard drive. As for my son, I'll take care of that situation. I need to think. But never, and I mean never, talk about it with me or anyone else, understood?"

"Understood," replied Yosef and Jacob.

Alon asked them to clean things up and then dispose of the bodies. He needed a long walk, and would get back to Rebecca's house on his own. In reality, he needed much more than a walk. He needed to resolve issues that no father should ever have to confront. He needed answers and for the present, he needed to not be alone with his son!

CHAPTER 29

Confrontation

An hour and half later, Alon arrived at Rebecca's home. The clock read 8:45 p.m. and the front porch lights were on, radiating beams of white light through the moderate snow as it fell to the ground. Alon, sick at heart, felt like vomiting from the acid build up in his stomach. What waited inside was going to be one of the hardest things any father could face. Standing in falling snow, he called Rebecca, who was still at work, and asked that she and her partner meet him at her house in about 30 minutes. He told her that he had important information that might solve the case. He would need those thirty minutes to talk with his son.

When he entered the house, both Sonya and Nadev were sitting on the couch watching a television program. He asked Sonya to please leave the house for about 20 minutes so that he and Nadev could discuss something in private. After a short protest she gave in and said that she'd come back later.

When she left, the two moved to Nadev's bedroom. They sat across from one another for several moments in silence. Alon had nothing prepared to say and could only stare at his son and ask, "Why? Why Nadev? My God, son, tell me why?"

"What are we talking about?" Nadev asked.

"We are talking about a young man who willingly and purposely plants and detonates a bomb in a restaurant, killing and injuring innocent people. We are talking about a coward who commits a violent act against society and then hides behind the claim that it was only in retaliation for previous political events. We are talking about a young man who not only

Day of Reckoning

disgraced himself and his country, but his family as well. As your father, I feel shame for all of us around you."

Nadev looked at his father's ashen face. For the first time in his life he saw the man weep in defeat and failure. "You're not my father!" he cried. "I am your biological offspring and that is all. We don't think alike, we don't act alike, and we don't see the world alike. You are an Israeli Jew who believes whatever you do is in the best interest of your western capitalist country. You can throw your military weight around because you have the financial and military support of the United States. I am an Islamic Jihadist. Yes, Islamic, who decided to push back against your aggressive oppression. You mean nothing to me so please don't offend me further by calling yourself my father."

Alon felt a stabbing pain in his gut. For once he had no words to say, and found it difficult to even look at the stranger sitting in front of him. When he did speak, he chose his words, realizing this was a life changing moment and there would be no chance of a replay.

"Nadev, when did this happen to you? I mean... are you a Muslim now? When? How? Why?"

Nadev answered as if he had rehearsed. "I was enlightened by what I learned through an Internet connection. I've been studying the Quran and other teachings of the prophet Mohammed for about two years. In answer to the 'why' part of your question, I would have to say it was because I was disgusted by the society I lived in."

"But how can you feel good about yourself and your beliefs knowing you have murdered thirteen innocent people, seriously hurt others, and created untold grief for their families? Where is your remorse?"

"Killing innocent people is an unfortunate by-product of any war, and believe me, we are at war. The explosion that day at Sid's Delicatessen was nothing more than a message from us to your western society. Keep supporting Israel in whatever it does, and we will continue to strike back. And you will all pay the price."

Anger rose in Alon. Where he had once felt speechless, his fighting energy returned. "Let me tell you something," he spat. "I agree...you are no longer a son of mine. The fact that you can cause such death and destruction without any remorse shows me you are diseased, your mind rotted by a radicalized ideology that has no place in human society. Don't think for a minute that you are a Muslim obeying the religious teachings of Mohammed. Islam is rich with peaceful teachings and you disgrace the Muslim name by saying you are one of them. You have been radicalized into thinking of yourself as a Jihadist, with a sacred duty blessed by God. In fact, you are nothing more than a small, misguided pawn in someone else's game."

"Fuck you, Alon!" Nadev said with hatred in his eyes.

"Here's the problem you now face. The two Iranians who supplied you with the C4 and training have been eliminated. I have collected the evidence of your involvement with them through email messages, personal recorded confessions, and cell phone contacts. In addition, I'm wearing a wire that has recorded our entire conversation." As Alon continued, he reached into his waist and pulled the wire so any further recorded conversation would not be included.

"In listening to your present views," Alon continued, "it's clear you feel nothing and regret nothing about what you've done. Therefore, I have no choice but to stop you. I'm going to turn over all evidence to the FBI. Now, think about this. You are an Israeli citizen. Israel will demand your extradition, and that will happen quickly, perhaps in a week or so. I can assure you that your return and conviction process will not be pleasant there. The Mossad will want to know all about your contacts, indoctrination process, and future anticipated operations. I will not be of any help and couldn't be even if I tried. At the very best, you will end up in a cell for the rest of your life. Need I tell you that those who operate the prison system in Israel and many prison inmates do not behave favorably towards those who put bombs in restaurants in the name of Islam. Radical Islamic Jihadism might be a new addition to your life, but you will see, it is a belief that will get very old, very quickly."

Nadev didn't say anything for a moment. He had no doubts where he stood in the judicial system of either country. "I take back nothing I've said or done," he said. "I am what I am, and feel no regret about any of it. You raised me, fed and clothed me, and cared for me for most of my life. But I will only ask you for one favor. If you feel anything for me, you will grant me this one wish."

"What is it?"

"I cannot be locked in a cell for the rest of my life. I would ask, beg, pray that you would give me one of those cyanide pills you told me

Day of Reckoning

Mossad agents frequently carry. Let me end my life with some dignity, not sitting in a cell staring at cement walls. Please, I beg of you. Give me a way out."

Alon sat stony faced across from his child. "Regardless of your warped views, you are still my son," he said, "and I can't facilitate your death. As a father, I just cannot do that!"

"I beg you grant me this one wish. Let me swallow a pill and escape what lies ahead. Do it as you would put an injured animal out of its misery. If you cannot do it as my father then do it as a Mossad agent who knows that given the chance, I will kill again. Do this thing for me, please. I ask nothing else."

Alon lowered his head and cradled it in his two hands. He wept, great racking sobs, moaning, "I can't do it. Oh, my God, I can't do it!"

"Alon, you have to help me with this. I am not asking for your forgiveness or your understanding, only for a small gesture of mercy. Give me the only way out I can endure. In the name of your God and beliefs, for our family, and for the knowledge that I am truly proud of what I have done, help me leave this world as the man I want to be."

With tears running down his face, Alon popped open a ring on the fourth finger of his left hand and poured the white powder it contained into a half-filled glass of water that sat on the table next to the bed. "It works fast," he said, "If you want it, take it now, before the FBI agents arrive."

Nadev reached for the glass.

"Wait! I forgot. Sonya will be back soon." For a moment Alon scarcely breathed. Then he made a decision. "I know how much the two of you mean to each other and before this terrible thing happens I will give you a chance for a few last minutes together. What you tell Sonya will be up to you. She is your sister and she loves you very much. What you say will be her last memory of you. Think before you speak."

"Thank you," Nadev replied. There was no 'dad,' 'father,' or I love you attached. Just a simple, thank you.

Chapter 30

No sooner had Alon and Nadev concluded their discussion when the front door opened and Sonya called out playfully, "Sonya Levy back in the house. Ready or not!"

Alon called out to his daughter to come back to Nadev's bedroom. When she entered, she sensed the tension in the room. "What's up, you two?" she asked.

"Your brother has something he wants to say to you," Alon said. He left the room, closing the door behind him and went to the living room to wait for the arrival of Agents Cramden and Kurnitz. In just a few moments, he heard a cry of disbelief, then Sonya's shouts of anger, fear, and remorse along with hysterical crying. Much as he wanted to go into the bedroom and comfort his daughter, Alon felt it was better for her to hear Nadev's story and deal with it directly. As he sat lost in his own thoughts, the two agents entered the house.

"Alon," Rebecca inquired, "what do you have for us?"

Alon started his story by establishing Walid Kassab's innocence. He explained in great detail why the young man had run, why he had given false identification, and what he needed to cover up from his past. "I have Walid in my personal custody and am ready to turn him over to you. Can you assure me that once his innocence is proven, he will not be deported and that he can keep his scholarship?"

Rebecca answered that although the final decision was not theirs to make, they would go to bat for Walid if he were indeed innocent.

Finally, Rebecca asked the golden question. "Then...who was the terrorist bomber?"

Alon started to choke up and once again, tears of emotional pain started to flow. He looked at Rebecca and gave her the answer he never thought he would say. "The terrorist bomber was my son, Nadev Levy."

Rebecca's jaw dropped. She stared at Alon, speechless. Cramden, in a more objective and practiced manner, asked Alon if Nadev was in the back room. Alon nodded his head affirmatively and watched as Agents Cramden and Kurnitz drew their weapons and approached the back bedroom. Cramden called, "Nadev, FBI agents coming in."

Alon leapt to his feet. "Stop!" he called as he rushed toward them. "Sonya is in that room. Let me bring her out first. I have been with Nadev. He's not armed. Please, I know about standard procedures and no one is in harm's way. I swear it!"

"Alright", Rebecca said. "Get her out quickly."

Alon knocked twice on the door. "Sonya, you need to come out now. FBI agents are here to take Nadev into custody." He entered the room. "Nadev, do not make any sudden or jerky moves. Just do as you are told."

As the two agents stood by the door Sonya left the room. Nadev grabbed the glass of water and gulped its contents. No sooner had Cramden secured Nadev's hands behind his back and secured them with handcuffs, Nadev buckled over, vomited violently, and fell to the ground in a fetal position. Sonya screamed. Alon got on the floor and held Nadev in his arms. Cramden unlocked the handcuffs, but it was too late to make a difference. Nadev lay on the ground, his eyes open, his pupils dilated, and his mouth exuding a thick white foam. Rebecca leaned down and put two fingers on Nadev's neck to determine a pulse, but felt nothing. The boy was dead.

"God dammit to hell, what just happened here?" Rebecca asked. "Alon, tell me you had nothing to do with this!"

Tears streamed down his face. His mouth moved, but no words came as he sat on the floor holding his dead son. As Cramden reached over to separate the two, Alon said in an icy undertone, "Keep your fucking hands off my son or I'll break them."

Rebecca told Cramden to back off and give Alon a few moments with Nadev. When he was ready, Alon rose to his feet. He released his hold on his son and retreated to the living room where Sonya sat sobbing on the couch. Alon sat beside her, took her in his arms, and let his tears join hers.

The agents stayed in the bedroom as they called in the local authorities and the federal forensic specialty team. By the time they emerged, Alon and Sonya had wiped away their tears and composed themselves. Agent Cramden walked over and extended his hand to Alon. "I'm sorry for your loss, Mr. Levy; I really am," he said. "And I'm sorry if I upset you in the room there. I was just trying to do my job."

Alon shook his hand and replied, "I know."

Rebecca went to the couch and sat between father and daughter. She put a consoling arm around Alon, and with her other hand, intertwined her fingers with those of Sonya. "I'm sorry Alon and Sonya. So very sorry," she repeated. "There are going to be a lot of questions. Right now, you two do whatever you need to do and just know I'm here to help you."

Funeral arrangements for Nadev were made, but could not be finalized until the scheduled autopsy had been completed. Alon fought the autopsy on religious grounds. He lost out legally to a questionable cause of death, perhaps homicide. Alon's plans were to leave, when allowed, to bury Nadev in Israel. Sonya would remain in Chicago and finish her academic program. She was hurt and shocked beyond description at the news of her brother's involvement. However, Sonya was a resilient child and Alon felt confident that given enough time, she would recover from the trauma. Walid was acquitted of any wrong doing. He received a lengthy lecture by a federal judge on the seriousness of fleeing a crime scene when asked to stay for questioning and giving false identification.

After the coroner delivered the autopsy report, Alon Levy found himself seated in a conference room before a federal judge, Agents Cramden and Kurnitz, an assistant prosecuting attorney, an appointed criminal defense attorney, and the director of citizen affairs from the Israeli embassy. Alon was shown the autopsy report indicating the cause of his son's death as cyanide poisoning. When asked about his complicity, either in supplying or directing his son to ingest poison, he denied any connection.

The prosecuting attorney signed a short release document and announced that no charges would be filed against him. He was free to leave. He shook hands, said his good-byes, and left for Sonya's apartment to complete his remaining business.

Rebecca approached Alon outside the building on his way to the parking lot. She offered to drive him to the airport the following morning, or help with transportation arrangements for Nadev, if needed. Alon informed her that the casket was en route to the airport. He thanked her and accepted the offered ride to O'Hare the following morning. There was much more he wanted to say, yet could not. He knew he would never be able to fully repay her generosity, kindness, and understanding during these last difficult months, but he wanted to try. Alon decided that once back in Israel, he would write a personal letter to each family affected by the death of a loved one in the bombing, apologizing for his son's actions. He hoped it would help bring closure, as well as letting them know that he, Alon Levy, cared deeply about their loss.

Alon's greatest concern was the emotional and psychological impact on Sonya of her brother's role in the bombing and his subsequent suicide. She insisted on finishing her education at the University and promised to maintain her friendship with Rebecca. Though she found Nadev's role in the bombing despicable, she also loved him, and would think of him always as her big brother.

In their private moment before his death, Nadev had explained to Sonya how he had begged for the cyanide, and in his own way was grateful to Alon for giving it. He swore her to secrecy about how he had obtained it. His final remarks were something he would never have said to his father. He asked his sister to forgive him, not for his beliefs, but for having done what he did. She kissed him good-bye and told him that she would always love him.

Chapter 31

Rebecca Kurnitz sat at her desk preparing to write her version of the summary report on the restaurant bombing. Her thoughts were interrupted by a soft knock on the door.

Her partner, Richard Cramden entered the office and sat down facing her. "Rebecca, what the hell really happened at your house the day Alon's son died? And what do I put in my report about it?"

"Look, Richard, all we know for sure is that Nadev committed the crime, lost his arm in the process, and took his own life to avoid deportation, and life-long incarceration. Your crime report should summarize the actual evidence and factual information into a more concise and palatable version for review. That's what a summary report is for."

"Come on. I believe Alon played some part in his son's death, don't you? And if he did, we have a responsibility to mention it."

"Actually, I do not, and I'll tell you why. First of all, Alon was nowhere near the boy when he took the lethal dose. You saw that. We both did. The coroner's report is in and the judge's ruling clears Alon. Nadev's death was a suicide. If you want to go against the judge's ruling and argue that the father supplied the cyanide, then go ahead and good luck. It's unnecessary conjecture, and you know how Director Jenkins reacts to that sort of thing. Anyway, what difference does it make? The kid planted the bomb and chose to die rather than spend his life in prison. A host of innocent people died and or had their lives changed forever because of this terrorist act. Is it really wrong for someone to provide a family member with the means to end his or her life following a confession of guilt in such a crime? Maybe some would say it depends on the circumstances. And if it were true in this case, it might be seen as a

Day of Reckoning

kind of justice. Now go back to your office and think about what you might have done if you were in Alon's situation. Write your report, and maybe leave out the speculation."

Agent Cramden nodded and got up to leave. He patted Rebecca on her shoulder as if to say thanks. As he left, he closed her door leaving her once again with her thoughts. Rebecca had a strong feeling about what probably took place that day, but she would never mention or refer to it in her report. As far as she was concerned, the case was closed.

An hour later, her finished report was ready for delivery to her boss, Director Jenkins. Rebecca walked with it down the hallway. Jenkins was seated at his desk and motioned for Rebecca to take a seat. She sincerely hoped he would not assail her with another session of negative criticism because she was not in the mood.

"Agent Kurnitz," he said, "I want to congratulate you on how you managed this case. Your work was methodical, comprehensive, and productive. You performed well as a team leader and I was proud of how you accumulated and interpreted your evidence data."

"Thank you, Director Jenkins," she replied. "I appreciate your feedback. I do want to make the point that Agent Cramden and the rest of the team also did an excellent job."

"So noted. However, on future cases there is one area that could use improvement—establishing emotional ties to outsiders involved in the case. I'm referring to your having that Israeli consultant and his two children, one of whom was the actual bomber, as guests in your home! Before the son was discovered, their presence could have led to emotions that may have compromised your objectivity. Do you follow me?"

Rebecca knew exactly what he meant and simply agreed by nodding her head.

"You don't have any sort of relationship with that man or his daughter now, do you?"

"No. They are no longer staying with me," she said. "I offered my home as a security measure after their apartment's security had been breached. It's now safe and they moved back into the daughter's apartment. While they stayed with me I enjoyed their company and appreciated Mr. Levy's knowledge of terrorism. Obviously, his son's involvement was a great surprise to everyone, including his father."

"Enough said. Let's end this discussion on a high note. You did well...very well, and I and the entire department are proud of you."

CHAPTER 32

Agent Kurnitz's Home in Chicago

The next two days found Alon Levy in a quiet, depressed, and withdrawn mood. He sat alone in the guest room of Rebecca Kurnitz's house sitting in a recliner staring out of the window at who knows what. Alon's mind wandered from topic to topic but always came back to the nightmare involving his son. He knew that Nadev's act of terrorism was unconscionable and he also realized that not only did his son feel no remorse but that this terrible act would be a stepping stone to others in time. Alon kept telling himself that he had had no legitimate options and that he had willingly complied with Nadev's wish for a merciful end. The thought though that did not stop haunting Alon and probably would for the rest of his life was the fact that he was still Nadev's father and assisting him to die just wasn't an acceptable part of his life.

Alon had no appetite for food, conversation, or even for thoughts of his upcoming return trip to Israel. He kept fixating on his earlier short comings as a father and somehow looking to blame himself for his son's actions. The father-son relationship was never a good one but maybe their strong ideological differences should have set off an alarm earlier or warning signal for things possibly to come. But then, just as Alon would start to fall into the dismal abyss of self-condemnation, he would snap back into a brief window of reality. After all was said and done, Nadev had made choices and those decisions involved committing an act of overt terrorism that ended the lives of several and changed the lives of many. Alon kept sitting in the recliner just staring out the window perhaps looking for answers that would never come.

Rebecca and Sonya were both sitting across from each other in the kitchen making small talk at the granite island counter in the center of the room. They had both tried to talk to Alon but the time was not right and the open wound too raw. The door to the guest room opened and Alon came into the kitchen for a glass of milk. Sonya was the first to speak and inquired as to how he was doing. Alon looked up and remarked, "I'll be fine. How about you?"

"I'll be o.k. Dad. It's just that I never saw any of this coming. Did my brother really hate our way of life so bad that he would do such a thing?"

"I don't know Sonya," was the reply. "I can only guess that his inner feelings were so vehement regarding our political, religious and social differences that he searched for an alternative answer. Maybe I should have been there more for him when he most needed it. Maybe I should have addressed his heart felt differences more thoroughly and certainly, with more sensitivity than I did. I don't know Sonya. I guess sometimes I wonder if anything would have mattered."

Rebecca then interjected her thoughts on the matter. "Alon," she began. "You cannot carry the weight of Nadev's actions on your shoulders alone. It's not fair to you or Sonya. He chose a path that apparently met his needs. He carried out an action that impacted a large group of people. He selected a commitment to a radicalized way of life that meant that this incident would probably prove to be one of many. You and your daughter share no blame or responsibility for those choices. I know that as a parent, you obviously feel a great loss but you had nothing to do with his ideological beliefs or plan of action."

"Deep down, Rebecca, I know what you say is true," Alon replied. "But it just hurts so much right now that words can't describe the way I feel. I'm sure that in time, things will make more sense and life will go on as it was but for right now, things seem to be pretty messed up."

Rebecca gently put a hand on Alon's forearm and said, "Alon, you'll be alright in time. I just know it. And Sonya, you too will heal and will always have the good memories of your brother with you as long as you live."

The two girls ate a light dinner together in the kitchen while Alon returned to the guest room to finish packing for his return trip. But after a few minutes, all was quiet in the room and Alon Levy had once again returned to the recliner and to his staring out the window at peaceful nothingness.

Alon's flight from O'Hare was scheduled for departure at 11:20 a.m. but of course, he was packed and ready about a day in advance. He had said his goodbyes to agent Cramden, Yosef, Jacob and Walid. Alon and Sonya spent a very enjoyable and private dinner together the night before the scheduled departure and then they both stayed up late reminiscing old times and discussing their unawareness of Nadev's involvement with such a radicalized political group. They cried together, recalled old times, and held each other to comfort their sorrows. Alon insisted that Sonya not accompany them to the airport because she had an exam that morning at school. They would stay in touch and see one another soon, either in Israel or back here in Chicago.

At about 8:30 a.m., the doorbell rang at Rebecca's house and when Alon answered it, Walid was standing on the front porch.

"Walid," Alon said with some measure of surprise. "What's up? Are you missing me already?"

Walid replied, "I guess I do. But what I really came over for was to express again how sorry I am for your loss. I also want to say a special thanks for helping me so much and for going to bat for me regarding my scholarship and continued education here in the States. I'm never going to forget you Mr. Levy and I hope you have no objections to my continued friendship with Sonya."

Alon smiled and said, "Walid, I am both honored and proud to call you a friend and feel much better knowing that you and Sonya are close to one another. Treat her good and look after her well Walid, and I'll appreciate that. Step out of line and I'll come and visit you."

The two of them laughed, shook hands, and then hugged each like family members. Alon turned back into the house to get his things since he needed some extra time to finalize some written arrangements regarding the air travel transfer of Nadev's body and casket to Israel. Rebecca was already in the kitchen taking small sips of hot coffee from a mug waiting for Alon to leave. The two of them packed the car and began the 35 minute ride to the airport.

The day featured a clear sky, a temperature of about 37 degrees, and a low to non-existent wind chill factor. Traffic was light but O'Hare was busy as usual even though it was a weekday. Alon took care of the required applications, certifications, and travel papers and then joined Rebecca at a coffee shop located just prior to entering the designated airport security check point. Alon reached out and put his hand on top of Rebecca's. "Becky," he began. "I'll never be able to thank you enough for what you've done for my family. This is a small token of my appreciation." And with that comment, Alon handed Rebecca a blank white envelope.

"I hope you use it," he said.

She opened the envelope to find an open ended round trip ticket voucher to Israel. It was business class travel and was good at any time within the next 12 month period.

"Oh my god," she exclaimed. "This is wonderful Alon. You didn't have to do anything like this but I sure am happy that you did. Of course I'll use it. You can count on that!"

"The part I left out Becky, is that you can stay as long as you want and you are my personal guest with no expenses. You'll stay at my place hopefully and I'll show you Israel like you deserve to see it. We'll have a great time together. I'll guarantee it!"

"I was hoping that you'd say something like that Alon and I accept your wonderful offer with all my heart and with that, she leaned over, hugged him and gave him a nicely placed affectionate kiss. Rebecca then asked Alon if she could ask him a few sensitive questions and then promised to never bring them up again. He told her of course and awaited her last-minute unofficial interrogation.

"What was it initially that made you suspect Nadev of committing such a crime?" she asked.

"Becky," he replied, "I swear to you, there were several odd signals along the way that in retrospect should have set off a wake-up call but they didn't. Perhaps, it is a question of parental denial but I never really suspected Nadev of committing such a crime and in fact, would never think him capable of ever considering such a radicalized affiliation."

"What were some of the warning signs now that you look back, that might have triggered concerns?" she continued.

"Nadev and I always had different ideological views of Middle Eastern politics. We had a strained relationship and I should have paid closer attention to what he was thinking, who he was communicating with, and how strongly he felt. Another warning sign was the forensics study by you people that showed bits and pieces of charred canvas material concentrically located away from the table where he was originally seated. Before going to the restroom, he put his back pack on the back of the chair. That was a tip that I should have focused in on but did not... The bomb was most likely in his back pack."

"Well," she replied. "You can't beat yourself up over denying your son's involvement. Most any parent would have done the same. If you never saw it coming, it would naturally be a tremendous shock that would be met with denial. Who, as a parent, would ever initially suspect their own child of such an act?"

"You know Becky," Alon began. "Thanks for the pep talk but the way I see it is that it also comes down to some bad or inadequate parenting on my part. I'll never fully convince myself that I shouldn't have recognized some of these signs and maybe could have addressed them earlier and more effectively. A lot of people died and many more scarred for life because of this misguided, uncontrolled, misfit that was, by name anyway, my son. I'll always feel some of the responsibility for what he did but for now, it's time to pick up the pieces and live life."

"Amen to that Alon," Rebecca replied.

"Another question that I have is, what is your final read on the assassination attempt at Sonya's apartment?"

Alon hesitated for a moment and then replied. "Knowing what I know now makes that event much clearer. In retrospect, I was never the intended target. Someone had ordered the assassination of Nadev to bury any information that he may have had regarding the planning and execution of the terrorist act. Let's face it. Suicide bombers are generally not intended to survive their assigned tasks. A survivor can talk and they, whoever they are, would never want that."

"Oh, and by the way," Rebecca said. "One last simple question and you can board the plane in peace."

"What's that my dear Becky?" he said.

"We cannot seem to locate those two Iranians and no one has heard from them during the last week or so. We got an order for a search and entered their apartment the other day. No sign of either of them but some blood smears on one of the walls and a section of carpet next to the couch. Now Alon, please tell me that you don't know anything about that business and I'll buy it."

Alon looked at her with that childish smile of his and said, "I absolutely had nothing to do with anything but if I were a betting man, I would say that the two of them will never again be a threat with supplying explosives to couriers in the Chicago area or anywhere else, ever again."

"Alon," she replied. "I love you but get out of here before I start asking more questions. I'll see you soon in Israel."

THE END

ACKNOWLEDGMENTS

My profound thanks to my editor, Lois Winsen, my manuscript coordinator, Jennifer Zupke, and the many readers who reviewed the earlier editions paving the way to improvements. Thanks, too, to the team at Self-Publishing Relief for so expertly guiding me through the process of transforming my manuscript into a published book.

Made in the USA
Lexington, KY
12 September 2016